DEATH'S
CLENCHED
FIST

Books by James Sherburne

A Paddy Moretti Mystery

DEATH'S
CLENCHED
FIST

James Sherburne

Boston
Houghton Mifflin Company
1982

Library of Congress Cataloging in Publication Data

Sherburne, James, date
Death's clenched fist.

I. Title.
PS3569.H399D39   813'.54   81-7205
ISBN 0-395-31835-1   AACR2

Printed in the United States of America

S 10 9 8 7 6 5 4 3 2 1

To the Garners
and Perkinses of Des Moines

—may their tribe increase

Contents

DEATH'S
CLENCHED
FIST

1

Diverse Encounters
with Three Women

As nearly as I can figure it out, the whole business started
with Joseph Pulitzer. If Pulitzer hadn't let himself be persuaded
to hire a woman reporter, then Nellie Bly would never have begun
her career in the Fourth Estate. Which means she would never
have developed her penchant for journalistic stunts, such as in-
terviewing murderers, circling the globe in less than eighty days,
and getting herself committed to Blackwell's Island as a certified
lunatic. Which, in turn, means she would not have approached
me to help her in one of her more harebrained stunts, and I
would not have been barred from McSorley's for six weeks, and
thus reduced to drinking at places like Tough Mike's.

It is almost impossible to say no to Nellie Bly— or to Liz
Cochrane, which is her real name — so I can understand Joseph
Pulitzer's problem. But understanding is not forgiving. He was,
after all, the man in the crucial position, and the responsibility
for his failure under stress must remain with him alone.

Liz accosted me in Lüchow's as I was eating a lunch of bratwurst and sauerkraut. "Paddy," she said firmly, "I need your help.
I intend to destroy an obsolete feudalistic tradition and I can't do
it alone."

"You mean the *World* needs another stunt story?" I pulled out a chair for her. "Sit down and tell me. But go easy on the bratwurst."

She sat down, planted her elbows on the table, and rested her chin on her tiny fists. She regarded me levelly from very wide, very blue eyes. "Paddy, what do you think of a public establishment that, in this enlightened era and in this cosmopolitan city, arbitrarily and unfeelingly denies admittance to women."

I considered the question. "I guess I would have to say I have mixed feelings. Which establishment were you thinking about?"

"McSorley's—your home away from home, I understand," she announced in a challenging tone.

"McSorley's?" I repeated. "*Of course* McSorley's keeps women out, Liz! Saints preserve us! Old John McSorley would rather serve a ring-tailed baboon than a woman! The very idea of a woman in McSorley's is scandalous to the point of blasphemy!"

Liz nodded her comely head. "It's exactly because of that attitude that I intend to drink a glass of beer there. The place is a bastion of prejudice. When it falls, the sound will be heard across the nation."

"Or at least any place where the New York *World* is read," I amended. "Please, Liz, forget it. Go to the bottom of the ocean in a diving bell—rescue a missionary captured by cannibals—jump off Brooklyn Bridge with Steve Brodie—but please stay the hell out of McSorley's Saloon."

"No doubt you're wondering why I've selected you to accompany me, Paddy," she continued. "Very well, I'll tell you. First, because you work for a weekly sporting newspaper rather than a metropolitan daily, so there's no question of your trying to scoop me. Second, because you're a regular at McSorley's, and anyone you came in with would be accepted without question. Third, because I can offer you twenty dollars to help me and be reasonably sure you'll agree." She picked up a slice of bratwurst with her fingers and nibbled it delicately.

I expostulated with her in vain. Once a course was set in her mind, it admitted to no alteration; she was as suggestible as the law of gravity. Finally I agreed, under strict conditions: that she should drink her beer and leave McSorley's without disclosing her true sex; that my name should not appear in her newspaper account of the incident; and that my identity as her co-conspirator would be revealed only if required by subsequent legal action.

Two days later we met outside Cooper Union and walked down Seventh Street to McSorley's. Liz had her hair stuffed under a cap and was wearing a bulky jacket and a pair of dungarees that concealed her most obvious feminine endowments. Touching an artfully applied smudge of soot on her cheek, she asked, "How do I look?" in an unconvincing baritone.

"Keep your head down and don't say anything. I'll do the talking for both of us."

I opened the door and we entered the saloon. It was crowded, warm, and redolent of ale, tobacco, and sawdust. Old John McSorley was behind the bar. We approached him and I ordered two steins. "You'll like this ale, lad," I said in a comradely tone. "Ahhh—just look at that head, won't you?"

We lasted five minutes.

The unmasking occurred when Liz could not resist disagreeing with a burly laborer who was expressing his opinion about the natural inferiority of Ulstermen, the English, Jews, Negroes, Italians, Chinese, and women. His reply was to knock her cap off, causing her curls to cascade down over her shoulders. We immediately became the center of an incredulous and outraged circle.

"Why did you do it, Moretti?" Old John asked me as I was being frog-marched to the door.

"God, I don't know! Don't bar me for life, John! I swear I'll never break the rules again!"

He regarded me judicially as I was raised in the air by four pairs of hands. "Six weeks," he announced. "Six weeks—then

3

we'll see." I sailed through the door and landed in a snowdrift, where a moment later Liz Cochrane joined me. I sat up and shook dark gray snow out of my sleeves. "Was that the sound of a bastion of prejudice falling?" I asked bitterly.

"Unfortunate," Liz said, struggling to her feet. "I'm afraid that's the end of my story. I couldn't write it this way—the ending lacks dignity. Oh, well—" She smiled brightly at me, the perfect image of the plucky little lady who journeyed around the world in seventy-two days, six hours, and ten minutes. "Success would have no savor if we didn't also know the dejection of defeat. Don't you agree?"

*

During the days that followed—the last week in February and the first few days in March—I spent most of my evenings in search of a saloon where I could enjoy a fraction of the relaxing fellowship I had always found at McSorley's. I visited gang hangouts in the old Five Points neighborhood, dock workers' barrooms on Cherry and Water streets, Italian wine shops on Elizabeth Street, lobster palaces north of Madison Square, dance halls in the Tenderloin, and deadfalls like Billy McGlory's Armory Hall on Hester Street.

One dismal, sleety night I found myself on the Bowery at Fifth Street. My shoes were waterlogged and I was chilled to the bone. When I saw two men emerge from a doorway under a sign that read "ZUM GROBEN MICHEL," I headed for them without hesitation. "Pardon me, but is this a saloon?" I asked. "Could a man get a glass of beer and a bite to eat here?"

The two men recoiled from me as if I had said something shameful. One of them muttered a few words in a language I took to be German, and the other glared at me from red-rimmed eyes and pulled his coat collar up around his neck. They walked quickly away.

"The murtherin' weasels," said a voice by my elbow. "They're off to build a bomb to blow up God-fearing women and children, most likely." I turned to see a policeman beside me, a look of indignation on his broad Irish face. He gestured toward the doorway before us. "That Tough Mike's, it's a nest of vipers in there. If it was me, I'd put a padlock on the door before they blow us all up."

"Well, I think I'll get me a glass of beer while it's still open," I said, moving toward the door.

He put a heavy hand on my arm. "If that's the place where you do your drinking, I think I better take a good look at you. Come here under the light, me boyo." He drew me close to a fogged window and studied my face with angry eyes. "Just so's I'll know you when I see you in the line-up."

I pulled my arm away. "I don't plan on being in any line-ups, officer. And if there's no law against it, I'll have that beer now." He made no further effort to restrain me, and I entered the saloon.

Zum Groben Michel, or Tough Mike's, as the policeman called it, was a long, dark room occupying the ground floor of a tenement. Until my eyes adjusted to the smoky dimness, my impressions of the place were entirely auditory and olfactory; the sounds were disputatious voices that suddenly dwindled to whispers at my entrance, the rattle of glassware from one side of the room, and the pounding of an out-of-tune piano from the other; the smells were wet wool and stale sweat, beer, cabbage, chicken fat, cheap tobacco, moldering plaster, and sewer gas. I hesitated a moment, blinking my eyes against the acrid smoke, and then crossed to the bar that ran down the length of the room. The bartender moved toward me, and two customers sidled a foot farther away. "You want something?" he asked in a heavy, Teutonic voice.

He was a great brute of a man, over six feet tall and weighing close to three hundred pounds. He was completely bald, and a purple scar cut across his gleaming pate from one ear to the other. His neck, which bulged like a wrestler's thigh, was discolored by a birthmark that disappeared under the dense curly hair that began at his collarbone. His eyes gleamed like small pale buttons between the pads of fat above and below them.

"A stein of your best, bartender—and are you the Michel whose name is on the door?" I asked pleasantly.

He leaned a few inches closer to me, creating the impression of an avalanche about to fall. "Why you ask?" he rumbled.

"No reason but good fellowship, pure and simple," I assured him. "I'm a sociable person, and I think it's nice for a man to know who he's talking to. Now my name's Paddy Moretti, and many people think it's strange to have an Irish first name and an Italian last name. 'How in the world did you get an Irish name like Paddy when you come from a family with an Italian name like Moretti?' they ask me. 'You may well ask that question,' I tell them—" I stopped because the bartender had moved away down the bar and was drawing me a stein of beer, a look of intense disgust on his face. He returned with glass and smacked it on the bar. "One nickel," he growled.

I paid him and asked politely if there was a free lunch in the establishment. He pointed down the bar, and I carried my beer in that direction. The food was laid out on a table underneath a poster that showed a menacing clenched fist with a broken fetter falling from its wrist above the words "PROPERTY IS THEFT." The lunch was a dispiriting collection of summer sausage, kraut, saltine crackers, and sardellen, that caustic cousin of the uptown sardine whose persistent saltiness requires a quart of beer to wash away. I put a few crackers and a chunk of sausage on a plate of questionable cleanliness and carried it and my beer stein to an empty table.

As I ate and drank, I observed the patrons of Tough Mike's seated around me. Most of them were men, and many of them wore beards. Suits outnumbered working clothes, although the suits were mostly threadbare and out of style. Most eyes peered out from behind spectacle lenses, and the language spoken by the excitable voices seemed to be German as often as English.

I nibbled on my food and sipped my beer, being careful not to give the impression of eavesdropping. After a minute or two, the people around me seemed to accept my presence or at least ceased to be concerned about it. Voices increased in volume and fists began hammering tables. Everyone seemed to be criticizing someone else—Marx, Gompers, and Benjamin Tucker caught most of the invective, but Kropotkin, Bakunin, Malatesta, and Johann Most were by no means immune. There were many foreign words used even by those who argued in English— *attentat, lumpenproletariat,* and *apparat* were favorites—and the same words seemed to occur in disputes conducted in German, Italian, and Yiddish. The arguments were pressed with passionate enjoyment; it was obvious that they, rather than the beer, the free lunch, or the discordant piano barely audible above the din, were the attraction of Zum Groben Michel.

I ate slowly, enjoying the feeling of warmth returning to my clammy toes and spreading out from my belly. *It's not McSorley's,* I thought, *but at least a man can sustain life here.* I swallowed a mouthful of beer and wondered if the piano player knew "Believe Me if All Those Endearing Young Charms."

A young woman moved between the crowded tables toward me. I watched her idly, thinking that her pale thin face and hollowed eyes were poorly complemented by the garish rouge on her cheeks. She was wearing a black dress of some shiny stuff that emphasized the inadequacy of her angular figure, her small breasts and boyish hips.

I didn't realize she was headed for my table until she sat down beside me and said, "Lonesome, honey?" in an artificially husky voice. "You look like you need some company," she went on, touching one finger to the back of my hand. "Be a sport and buy me a drink."

I was surprised. "To tell you the truth, that was the farthest thing from my mind when I came in here," I said. "But I'd be delighted if you'd join me for a glass of beer."

I craned my neck to find a waitress. My companion laughed.

7

"You'll have to go get it yourself—Tough Mike don't believe in spoiling his customers."

I brought two steins back to the table and raised mine in salutation. "To your very good health," I said. She had her glass to her lips when she heard my words. She was seized by a convulsion of laughter which changed immediately to a racking cough. Beer sprayed from her mouth and dribbled down her chin. With her head lowered and shoulders hunched and one hand covering the lower part of her face, she fought the cough spasms. I leaned toward her and touched her shoulder. "Are you all right?" I asked in concern.

She threw her head back and stared at me wide-eyed. "Oh, I'm great, I'm wonderful. Look." She held up one hand, palm down and parallel to the tabletop. It trembled like a leaf in a high wind. "Only for Christ's sake buy me some whiskey. Please?"

I made another trip to the bar and returned with a bottle of rye whiskey and two small glasses. I filled one and handed it to her. She took it in both hands, threw the liquid down her throat, and held it out to be refilled.

"I'd say you needed that," I commented as I poured out more liquor.

"You'll never know." She emptied the glass again, shuddered, and set it down before her. "Now, where were we? I was telling you how you didn't have to be lonesome anymore, wasn't I?" She ran the tip of her tongue along her lips and raised one eyebrow theatrically.

I thought she looked like a sick little girl playing dress-up in her mother's clothes. "I think we should get something straight, Miss—what name might I call you by?"

"Maisie. And there's only one thing you need to get straight, and I'll take care of that for you. You get it?" She laughed and almost started to cough, but managed to suppress it. "That was a joke. Come on, honey, give me a smile." She picked up my hand in both of hers and tickled my palm with her finger. "In a little while you're going to have a lot to smile about."

"That's what I wanted to get straight," I said. "I'm not in the market. You're more than welcome to sit here and have a drink or two, but that's all there'll be for you."

Her eyes widened, and she pulled my hand toward her breast. "What's the matter, honey? Shy? Don't be." I disengaged my hand. "Is it the money? Don't worry about that. You got six bits? A dude like you, you got six bits, ain't you?" She reached for my hand again. "Hell, four bits'll be all right—I know how it is to be short. You got four bits—you *gotta* have four bits!"

"No, no, it's not the money!" I said quickly before she could lower her price any more. "It's—" I improvised, "it's a terrible misfortune that befell me. I caught a rare disease in the Far East—left me no more than the merest nub—a never-ending source of embarrassment and humiliation."

She stared at me a moment in disbelief, then slumped back in her chair. "Aw, you're lying, but the hell with it. If I ain't worth four bits, I might as well go to the Circus, I'm all washed up on the street." She stared numbly at the empty glass before her. I could see by the tightening of her throat muscles that she was fighting another spasm of coughing.

I poured her another drink and one for myself. "I'd consider it an honor if you'd stay and have a glass or two with me, Maisie. I always relish the company of a pretty woman."

She straightened her thin shoulders and reached for the drink. Then her mouth began to tremble, her eyes brimmed over, and lowering her head into her hands, she began to sob noisily. I leaned toward her in alarm. "Don't do that, now! Drink your drink, and things will look rosier. That's a girl!"

She shook her head blindly and her sobs grew louder. "Might as well go to the Circus," she repeated in a rising wail. "Might as well kill myself, get it over fast!"

I was aware that the sounds of spirited argument from the

surrounding tables had quieted. As I turned to see whether my distraught companion and I were the cause, a young woman standing behind me pushed her face into mine and said, in a strong, ominous voice, "What did you do to that girl, you bourgeois bastard?"

She was a small woman, but full-bodied, with light hair cut short and brushed to one side, penetrating eyes under heavy brows, and too wide a jaw. It was a face that seemed designed to show indignation. Behind her stood a young man with bat ears and a chest and shoulders too broad for his slight body.

The woman pushed past me and put her arm around Maisie's shoulders. "It's all right, you tell me now—what did this *momser* say to you? He asked you to do things? He made you indecent proposals?"

"Now, just a minute!" I said spiritedly. "The only thing I've done is buy this lady a number of drinks, after she asked me to!"

The short-haired woman turned on me furiously. "You shut up, you hear! Exploiter! You think everything is for sale from poor people! Sasha!" she cried to the bat-eared young man, "If he try to escape, knock him down!"

I looked at the circle of faces surrounding us and found no encouragement. I turned back to the short-haired woman, who was now stroking Maisie's arm and talking to her softly in a crooning voice. "You seem to be suffering under a misapprehension, madam," I said. "I didn't approach her, she approached—"

"Don't call me madam—I do not sell women to cater to your corrupt capitalist lusts! Sasha, Fedya, Ernst—," she called imperiously, "sweep this *dreck* out to the street!"

The bat-eared young man stepped purposefully toward me, and two other men moved forward behind him. One was long-haired but clean-shaven, with narrow shoulders and a pasty complexion; the other was squat and burly, wore a full beard, and seemed to be missing one eye. Bat Ears brought one hand down on the back of my neck and began to lift me by my coat collar, and a moment later the burly man seized my right arm and twisted it behind my back. The long-haired man took hold of my left arm indecisively. I thought, *The bum's rush from Mc-Sorley's, all right, I deserved it. But not, by God, from Tough Mike's!* I twisted my left arm free and sideswiped the long-haired man. Immediately the bruiser behind me wrapped his massive forearm around my neck and increased the pressure on my pinioned arm until it felt like it was coming free from my shoulder.

"*Raus, schweinhund!*" he rasped in my ear, as he twisted me around to face the door.

"No, wait! Don't throw him out! He didn't do nothing!" I heard Maisie cry behind me. "It's like he said, I was hustling him. He bought me a couple of drinks and God I needed them! I wouldn't want you to hurt him for that."

The pressure on my arm eased slightly as the short-haired woman said sternly, "You tell the truth? You don't just say it so he will pay you money?"

"He ain't going to pay me any money anyway—I already know that." She coughed. "Hell, let him go."

The short-haired woman sounded disappointed as she ordered her associates to release me. I turned around to face her, rubbing my shoulder gingerly. "Another minute of that and me and me arm would have parted company permanently," I said. "You and your friends are very determined people, mada—ma'am." I moved back toward my chair, but she blocked me with her stocky body.

"Who are you, bourgeois?" she demanded. "What are you doing at Zum Groben Michel?"

I told her my name and added that I belonged to the working press, not the bourgeoisie. "I'm an underpaid, overworked wage slave for *The Spirit of the Times*," I said.

"The horse race newspaper?" she asked.

Surprised at her recognition of a paper whose circulation was mainly among the well-to-do, I answered, "Oh, we're a bit broader based than that. The masthead says we're a Chronicle of the Turf, Field Sports, Aquatics, Agriculture, and the Stage. But the Turf part is the most important, you're right about that."

"So you work for *The Spirit of the Times*—that is interesting," she said thoughtfully. She stepped to one side. "Sit down, Mr.— What is your name?"

"Moretti, Paddy Moretti." I gestured to an empty chair. "Won't you join us? I'm sure Miss Maisie will be pleased, after the spirited defense of her virtue that you and your friends put up."

"I will sit with you. Sasha also. The others will leave." Immediately her wishes were put into action; the bat-eared young man sat down at our table, and the long-haired man and the bruiser gave abrupt little bows and returned whence they had come. She said firmly but kindly to Maisie, "You too, *golubchik* —you go too. Go home, go to bed. Stay warm."

Maisie's eyes widened. "But I—" She hesitated as she looked from one to the other of us, as if waiting for someone to countermand the order. Then she licked her lips and said in a low voice, "All right. That's what I'll do. Go home and go to bed. Alone." She turned her gaze on me. "Thanks for the drinks, mister. I'm sorry if I caused you trouble."

"No trouble. Good night, Maisie."

I watched her as she weaved her way through the crowded room, her dark hair lank on her shoulders, her ill-fitting black dress too tight at the waist and too loose at the hips. Some of the men at the tables tried to stop her as she passed by, but she refused them with a word or a shake of the head and continued toward the door.

"Do you think she'll go home—alone?" I asked the short-haired woman.

She shrugged her shoulders. "Perhaps. If she truly wants a man she should take a man. But I do not think she truly wants a man. And when a woman does not want a man, no man should touch her, for if he does, he is a tyrant and she is a slave, and he will be judged for it. My name is Marya Perlman, and my friend is Felix Algauer. I call him Sasha because he looks like a Sasha. Shall we have a drink of your whiskey?"

I filled the two glasses for my guests and poured two fingers into one of the empty beer steins for myself. "Up the rebels!" I said, raising my drink.

Marya and Sasha raised their glasses in response. "Up the rebels!" Marya repeated. "I drink happily to your toast."

"And I," said Sasha, throwing his drink down his throat in one abrupt movement.

My two new companions and I sat talking and drinking in Tough Mike's for over two hours, and we learned a good deal about one another as we emptied one bottle and lowered the liquor level of a second to half. They learned from me that I was half Irish and half Italian, that I had grown up in a village in southern Ohio, which I had left because of my obsessive desire to follow the horses, that I had become a racing writer almost by accident, but had remained one ever since, and that I had worked for *The Spirit of the Times* for the past six years. They learned about my generally disastrous relationship with my editor, Otto Hochmuth—Marya seemed particularly interested in the unhappy details. And they learned that I lived in a two-room flat on Bleeker Street, and that I was in Zum Groben Michel because I was barred from McSorley's for six weeks.

Marya put her hand down on mine. "Ah, *gospodin,* then you are a rebel too—a rebel against male tyranny! And for that you are denied the chance to drink with your friends and forced to visit this den of revolutionaries. You suffer for your ideals—how tragic, how inspiring!" Her eyes danced with mischief. I noted that her hand was red and rough, but warm.

Then she told me about herself. She was only twenty-one, although she looked and acted five years older. She had been born in Lithuania and raised in St. Petersburg, the middle child in a family of five. I gathered that her family life had been stormy; she felt her mother had always resented her, and her father wished she were a boy. She learned rebellion early—she refused to marry a man her father picked out for her when she was fifteen, and her father whipped her until she dropped to the floor, unconscious.

"You know what he said to me once?" she asked, raising her glass to the light and staring moodily through the dark liquid. "He found me reading my French grammar, and he took it away from me and threw it into the fire, and said, 'Girls don't have to learn things like that! All a Jewish daughter needs to know is how to prepare gefüllte fish, cut noodles fine, and give the man plenty of children!'"

Sasha snorted contemptuously. "Men like that will be swept aside. There is no room for them in the world that is dawning."

Marya had come to America in 1885 and joined her sister in Rochester, New York. She got a job in a garment factory for $2.50 a day, working for a German Jew who felt that Russian Jews were fair game. After a few months, she bowed to what she and all the society she knew considered inevitable—she married a persistent suitor, even though she did not love him. He proved to be impotent. "I cannot complain too much, *gospodin,*" she said with a self-mocking smile on her full lips. "I try to escape my life instead of to change it—this is the punishment I deserve. And for me it's a real punishment, hah, Sasha?" She grinned lecherously at her friend, who looked down at the table in embarrassment.

From what I gathered, Marya and Sasha lived together on the lower East Side. Apparently the long-haired young man called Fedya also shared their lodging; he was Sasha's cousin, but his relationship with Marya was unclear. They worked at a variety of jobs to keep bread on the table—Marya sewed silk waists on a sewing machine in her room for a nearby shirtwaist factory, studied and practiced nursing, and made speeches for whatever a passed hat would bring in; Sasha wrote articles for radical newspapers and cut felt for an East Side hatmaker; Fedya did occasional odd jobs in exchange for the freedom to spend most of his time painting, for he aspired to a career in fine art. The three of them had been living this way since Marya, freshly divorced from her frail reed of a husband, had found her way to New York City a year before.

They were, of course, anarchists, a fact that took me a while to get used to. In common with most Americans, I divided anarchists into two classes: there were the native American, literary kind, like Thoreau and Josiah Warren, who wouldn't harm a fly; and then there were the foreign-born kind who agitated the working class and threw bombs which often killed innocent bystanders. People had begun to become aware of the second kind of anarchists in 1881, when five of them assassinated Tsar Alexander II in St. Petersburg just about the time Marya Perlman was celebrating her unhappy twelfth birthday there. During the following decade, there had been assassinations and other outrages perpetrated by anarchists—they called them *attentats*— in most of the capitals of Europe. For Americans, the most alarming event had taken place in Chicago in 1886, when a handful of admitted anarchists were addressing a gathering of strikers at Haymarket Square. A bomb had been thrown among a platoon of advancing policemen, no one ever established or even suggested by whom, and in the ensuing explosion and gunfire, seven policemen and God knows how many strikers were killed. Seven anarchists were put on trial for murder. As a newspaperman not unacquainted with the criminal justice system, I realized that the prosecution did not produce a single piece of evidence connecting any of the defendants with the bomb throwing. So too must the judge and the jury have known—but in the hysteria of the moment all seven of the accused were condemned to death.

In the four years since then, the hysteria had changed to an abiding aversion. Anarchists were depicted in newspaper and magazine cartoons as degenerate, bloodthirsty madmen with spiky beards and pockets bulging with bombs. Established labor unions, Gompers's American Federation in particular, strove to establish their patriotism by the bitterness of their denunciation of anarchism, and clergymen of all denominations denounced it regularly from their pulpits.

Now I thought, as I looked across the scarred table at Marya's square jaw and stern brows, and at Sasha's stevedore neck and shoulders, *Jesus, Mary, and Joseph, what am I doing with these people?*

And yet, as the liquor went down in the whiskey bottle and the arguments at the surrounding tables increased in volume, I realized that I was becoming comfortable with my new companions. In fact, I was enjoying myself.

We discussed the subject of terrorism, naturally.

"Terrorism?" Marya said with an impatient shake of her head. "Who preaches terrorism? Bakunin? Kropotkin? No, my friend, no one advocates terrorism. Terrorism is an attempt to force a policy through fear; we anarchists wish to show the way to the masses so that they will freely choose to cast off their oppressors. We are guides, we are not criminals." Her voice was low-pitched and intense.

"Forgive me, but I was suffering under the delusion that you occasionally put bombs under grand dukes and prime ministers and such," I said.

She frowned as she shrugged her shoulders. "Sometimes there is violence, but we are responsible for much less than we are charged with by the kept press. But you must understand this, *gospodin;* we reject purely political action. We believe that the whole political system—the executives and the congresses and the judges, the cabinets, the courthouses, the *apparatchiks,* and the tax collectors—all, all is one complex device to exploit the worker. And politics cannot be changed by politics! The political process is a trap set by our enemies—only by substituting direct action can we hope to find justice and freedom!"

"Direct action means killing people?" I asked.

She closed her eyes for a moment as if gathering her strength. Sasha growled under his breath impatiently and poured more whiskey into his glass. Marya opened her eyes and stared at me with an expression that seemed to combine defiance with a plea for understanding. "For us there can only be the Propaganda of the Deed. We do not vote, so we must act. But direct action need not be assassination—it can be strikes, boycotts, industrial sabotage, the formation of cooperatives, passive resistance—"

"But it can be assassination too," I interrupted.

She hid her irritation with difficulty. After a moment, she raised her glass and sipped the raw liquor. "I am not used to whiskey—I must watch out or I will become tipsy and Sasha will have to put me to bed. Or someone will." She put her small, warm hand on mine again. "You said you live on Bleeker Street. You and the artists, hah? You are a Bohemian? Where on Bleeker Street do you live?"

I told her my flat was three doors east of Sixth Avenue, and that there were indeed a number of Bohemians living near me, but I would hardly consider myself one. What, no mad parties until the sun came up? she asked. No artists' models posing in the altogether, no poets who smoked opium? And no little *liebchen* who knew the meaning of the word *freedom?*

I shook my head ruefully. "I'm afraid it's a life of total dullness I lead, and you've put your finger on it exactly," I said.

"Marya, it's getting late," Sasha said suddenly.

Marya looked at me for a long moment, her lips parted and her eyes glittering. She slowly ran the fingers of one hand down her cheek, and her throat, until the tips of her fingers came to rest within the collar of her shirtwaist. "I like you, Paddy Moretti," she said, "you with your life of total dullness."

"Marya," Sasha repeated nervously, "it must be after eleven. We must go."

Marya sighed and leaned back in her chair. "You are right. If I do not want to become tipsy and perhaps foolish, I must go now." She rose from her chair, and Sasha and I stood up with her. Until then I hadn't realized how short she was; her head was a foot below mine. She smiled up at me. "Thank

you for the whiskey, Paddy Moretti. Perhaps we will meet again."
I said I hoped so. She raised her clenched fist. "Up the rebels!"
"Up the rebels!" I answered. I watched them until they disappeared from view among the drinkers standing near the street door.

I decided I didn't want to drink any more, so I carried the half-bottle of whiskey back to the baldheaded bartender and settled up with him. "It's a great place you have here," I said as I pocketed my change. "Is it always as lively as this?"

He leaned toward me, resting his weight on his two gigantic fists. "Why you ask?" he rumbled.

I sighed, gave him a wave, and headed for the exit.

2

The Squire of
Stillwater Farm Stables

THE SAD GRAY MONTHS of late winter and early spring are depressing enough for all New Yorkers, but for horse race reporters they are especially dispiriting, for there are no major racing meets anywhere in the region during this period. This means that we scribes of the Sport of Kings are forced to abandon our chosen field and write on any subject our editor assigns us in an attempt to justify our meager salaries. It also means we present an inviting target to every budget cutter hoping to prune an office payroll, and enhance his reputation in the process.

Shivering from the savage wind that whistled across the Hudson, I trotted along Chambers Street and turned into the door marked 101. The editorial office of *The Spirit of the Times* was still cold, although hot water was knocking in the radiators and some of the windows were already fogged with steam. I made my way through the early-week activity—bustling, but not yet frenzied—and hung up my overcoat on the rack near my desk. My next-desk neighbor, Bertram McAnly, whose personal traits as well as his professional duties on the aquatic sports staff had earned him the nickname of Bert the Barnacle, smiled at me smugly. "You're seven minutes late, Moretti, and Hochmuth has already asked where you were," he said with satisfaction.

I considered his well-scrubbed, closely shaved face and soft pink mouth with distaste, but decided it was the wrong time of year to create unnecessary dissension with a fellow employee. "Thank you, Bert, I appreciate it," I said politely. "My, you look good enough to eat this morning—would that be a new tie you're wearing?"

He glanced down at the mauve-and-mustard foulard carefully knotted around his fat neck. Its paisley pattern appeared to depict a battle royal between giant paramecia. "Oh, you like it? It is new, as a matter of fact. Quite assertive, but also quite chromatically harmonious, don't you agree?"

"Exactly what I would have said myself, if I had your facility with language," I answered. I selected a half-dozen dull pencils from the thirty-odd dull pencils standing in the beer mug on my desk and walked to the pencil sharpener. As I sharpened them, I covertly studied the unappetizing face of my editor, Otto Hochmuth, at his desk across the room.

As always, Hochmuth was wearing the green eyeshade which gave his complexion the hue that characterizes the faces of floaters after a week in the East River. His bulging eyes were fixed on a sheaf of copy paper in his hand, and his small mouth was pursed in a buttonhole of distaste. As he read, he scratched his scrawny neck with a nicotine-stained finger. One knee jiggled nervously as his high-topped black shoe tapped the floor in staccato rhythm. I sighed and tucked the sharpened pencils in my breast pocket; Hochmuth looked exactly as he did every working day of the year.

I drew myself up before him. "Good morning, Mr. Hochmuth. I do believe I caught the first smell of spring in the wind this morning. It can't be long now, can it?"

He lowered the papers in his hands and raised his eyes to my face. "Good morning, Mr. Moretti," he said in his high, expressionless voice. "Since you were outside more recently than anyone else in this office, I'll take your word about the weather."

He paused to allow me to respond; when I didn't, he went on: "I believe one of the harbingers of the vernal season is the opening of the Elizabeth race meet, is it not?"

"Yes, sir. Elizabeth is the first major East Coast meet. It's sort of a preliminary for Gravesend, Sheepshead Bay, and Monmouth. It begins on April fifteenth."

"And should you still be employed by this publication at that time, you would be present there, naturally."

I swallowed. "Yes, sir."

"Mr. Moretti, one of the owners who intends to race his horses at Elizabeth this year is Harrison Cobb, of Oyster Bay, Newport, and Bar Harbor. Mr. Cobb is a newcomer to the sport, and this season will mark the maiden appearance of his colors at the track. His very close friend—" Hochmuth paused and worked his mouth for a moment as if tasting an exotic flavor he couldn't classify and then repeated, "His very close friend, who is also the proprietor of this newspaper, Mr. Frederick Follinsbee Monk III, feels it would be an act of kindness as well as an astute piece of journalism to feature Mr. Cobb's stable in an article to be run just before the opening of the Elizabeth meet."

I gave a mental shrug which I was careful not to let dampen the enthusiastic expression I adopted. "That's a grand idea, surely, Mr. Hochmuth—we'll give Mr. Cobb a leg up in the racing game and show our interest in an up-and-coming new stable besides." *At least,* I thought to myself, *it will get me out of rewriting correspondents' stories about the lawn tennis championship in Palo Alto.*

"I'm delighted to have kindled your enthusiasm," Hochmuth said drily. He shuffled the papers in his hand and separated one sheet from the others. "Here are the pertinent facts. Mr. Cobb is expecting your visit, and I would be sorry if you disappointed him." He reflected a moment, and added, "Sorry—but not heartbroken beyond solace. There would be one great consolation." His knee began to jiggle as his high-topped shoe tapped the floor. "Good day, Mr. Moretti."

I returned to my desk and studied the paper he had handed me. It read:

STILLWATER FARM STABLES
Oyster Bay, L.I.
MR. HARRISON COBB, PROP.
(4 m. S. on Jericho Rd.)

I folded it and put it in my pocket. From the next desk Bert the Barnacle asked, "What did he want, Moretti? Did he give you what-for about coming in late?"

I chuckled. "What an idea, Bertram! As a matter of fact, he was asking my opinion on one or two stocks he expects to add to his portfolio." I lowered my voice. "I suggested that now was the time to sell, not buy."

Bert the Barnacle scowled. "Oh, you liar," he said. "Since you're not doing anything this week, I could use a little help on the Wilmington Regatta story." He began digging among the papers on his desk.

I explained that, although nothing would make me happier than to work side by side with him, I was forced to give priority to the assignment I had just received from Hochmuth. "So hold the fort, Bertram," I added earnestly. "More depends on you than you can ever know." I slipped on my overcoat and, whistling cheerfully, made my way through the noisy room to the street outside.

*

I arrived at Stillwater Farm Stables, Mr. Harrison Cobb, Prop., a little before noon. The sun had broken through the slaty clouds during the morning, and my ride from the train station in a hired hack was very pleasant. The first birds of spring raised their voices tentatively in the crisp air, and there was a faint green tint that overlay the tired brown grass and foliage beside the road. The manor house at Stillwater Farm was a stately red brick

building of Georgian design, with a classical colonnaded porti-
co jutting out the front like the cowcatcher on a locomotive. I
knocked on the massive door with a heavy brass knocker shaped
like a roaring lion's head. After a few moments it opened to reveal an elderly Negro in butler's livery. He frowned disapprov-
ingly and asked, "Yes, what is it?"

"I'm Moretti, from *The Spirit of the Times*. I believe Mr.
Cobb is expecting me." He looked me over from head to foot,
and I had no doubt that if it had been his decision to make, he
would have sent me around to the kitchen entrance. But he swung
the door wide and said grudgingly, "Follow me, please."

We walked through a tiled foyer and a formal sitting room
with gilt-framed landscape paintings on the walls, continued down
a short hall lined with sporting prints of flat races and steeple-
chases, and paused before a closed white door. The butler opened
it and announced, "Mr. Moretti, the man from the racing newspaper, sir."

The room I entered looked more comfortable than the sitting
room. Five people turned toward me and one of them rose from
his chair and offered his hand. "How do you do, Moretti," he
said in a deep, authoritative voice. "I'm Harrison Cobb. How's
my good friend Fred Monk these days?"

We shook hands; his grip was firm, although the flesh of his
hand was soft. "He was fine the last time I saw him, although
we're not exactly daily companions," I answered.

"No, I don't suppose you would be," he said offhandedly. With
a wave of his hand he began introductions. "My dear, this is
Fred Monk's man Moretti—Moretti, Mrs. Cobb." I bowed to
a bony, gray-haired woman who appeared to be at least ten years
her husband's senior, and she smiled pleasantly if vaguely in reply. "Mrs. Kanady, Mr. Kanady, Mr. Moretti," Cobb continued;
the man and woman seated together on a green brocade couch
acknowledged my presence with perfunctory nods. She was a
pretty woman of thirty-five or so, with an Irish colleen kind of
coloring that had been thrown out of balance by too much rouge

and powder. Her husband was handsome in a coarse, ruddy way, although his jowls and neck were running to fat. Something about him, his name or his appearance, stirred a faint chord of memory. "And Mr. Terhune," Cobb concluded, gesturing to a slim, blond man in an elegantly tailored light gray suit, who sat in a leather wing chair with one gleaming shoe resting carelessly on the other knee.

The name Terhune reinforced the chord of memory, and I realized who the two men were. *Tammany Hall.* Tim Kanady was one of the leaders of the assembly districts who made up Tammany's Executive Committee, the second level of control that functioned directly beneath Richard Croker, the leading sachem of the New York Democratic organization. And Eddie Terhune, I remembered, was a City Hall lawyer with a reputation as one of Tammany's fastest rising young stars.

I returned Terhune's nod with a bow. "It's a great pleasure to meet you, ladies, gentlemen," I said.

I noticed that all five of them had glasses of one sort or another in their hands, but Cobb made no move to offer me anything. Rather, he drew a wafer-thin gold watch from his vest pocket and glanced at its face. "It's almost twelve. All the horses should be back in their stalls by now," he said. "What do you say we walk down, Moretti? I can give you some background on Stillwater Farm Stables on the way, and then I can show you some of the horses."

Realizing that no drink was going to be offered me, I agreed with a show of enthusiasm. Cobb invited the others to join us. His wife smiled wanly and refused, but Kanady agreed immediately. "Come on, Flo," he said as he rose from the couch, clapping his meaty hands together, "stop trying to fill that hollow leg and let's get some fresh air."

His wife frowned in irritation. "Really, Tim, how many times have I told you the genteel word is *limb,* not *leg*?" She emptied her wine glass and set it down on the rosewood table beside her. As she rose, Kanady turned to Eddie Terhune. "Come on, counselor—if you're not scared of getting some horse shit on your shoes," he said challengingly.

Terhune gave Kanady a mocking look. "Since you've been heading the Streets and Sanitation Committee, that's something every citizen of New York City has had to worry about," he said. "However, I can use the fresh air." He uncrossed his legs and rose from his seat.

Flo Kanady said to Cobb's wife, with a gesture of defeat, "I just hate the way Tim talks, but there's nothing I can do about it. He just won't listen to me." Mrs. Cobb smiled slightly and lowered her eyes, as if to acknowledge the common helplessness of the gentler sex.

"All right, let's go," Cobb commanded, leading the way out of the room and through the back of the house. We came out through a kitchen garden to a lane that led back to the stables. The main stable building and the adjacent outbuildings gleamed in immaculate coats of new white paint. Above each entrance was a painted coat-of-arms two feet wide and three feet high, which showed a horse's head, nostrils flared and mane tossing, above a shield quartered into purple and green sections, with a scroll beneath which bore the modest words, *Veni, vidi, vici.* Cobb explained its significance to me: "The horse's head signifies racing, naturally. Purple and green are my colors—purple for the Sport of Kings, green for the greenbacks I expect to win. Those words underneath, they're Latin—they mean 'I came, I saw, I conquered.' It's a quotation from Julius Caesar."

"Oh," I said.

We entered the stable and walked down the center aisle. Many of the stalls on either side were empty; although the building had been built to accommodate forty horses or more, there were scarcely half that many here. Cobb explained, "You know it takes time to build a great stable, Moretti, and that's just exactly what I intend to do. So I don't buy horses just to buy horses—I buy them to win races. And I've got all the time in the world."

We made our way down the aisle slowly, as Cobb commented

on each horse we passed, Kanady joked about its prospects, and I made notes in my notebook. Terhune and Mrs. Kanady had fallen fifteen or twenty feet behind. In front of one stall, I paused as a small chestnut horse nuzzled my palm with a velvet muzzle. "Say, you're a friendly one," I said. "I'm sorry I don't have anything to give you." I patted his glossy neck with my hand.

At that moment, a short, bandy-legged man in britches and boots appeared at my elbow. "Damned beggar!" he said hoarsely, putting his hand against the horse's nose and pushing its head back into the stall. The chestnut tossed his head and looked reproachful. I noticed a small, pinkish growth, a wart or wen, just at the corner of his right eye. The bandy-legged man turned to Cobb. "That horse is too friendly, Mr. Cobb. You shouldn't ought to encourage him," he said accusingly. "Friendly horses don't win races."

"You're right, Matt, you're right," Cobb chuckled tolerantly. "Hard to be rough on them when they just want to show you they love you, though." He turned to me. "Moretti, I want you to meet my trainer, Matt Wallens. Moretti's one of Fred Monk's reporters on *The Spirit of the Times,* Matt. They're going to do a write-up on us before the Elizabeth meet."

Wallens shook hands with me. His face, above the hairy black turtleneck sweater he wore, was wide, flat, and scored by sullen lines running downward from eyes and mouth. "Matt Wallens," I repeated. Something about him was familiar, but it wasn't his name. "Have we met before?"

He dropped my hand. "Maybe at some track somewhere. I've been around."

"I like this stallion here," I said conversationally. "What's his name?"

Harrison Cobb answered. "Bonnycastle—sired by Hittite out of Fandango. I got him in Kentucky last spring, from the Alexanders at Woodburn Farm. He's a grandson of Lexington!" Since Lexington was generally considered the greatest sire in the history of American racing, I could understand his obvious pride. However, it seemed to intensify the sourness of Matt Wallen's expression.

"Breeding's not everything, Mr. Cobb," he said. "A horse has got to want to win so bad he's willing to half-kill hisself to do it. Nobody knows if this one wants it that much. Especially if people keep spoiling him."

Cobb explained to me, "Most three-year-olds have run a few races before they turn three, but we had to keep Bonnycastle on the sidelines last fall because of a muscle strain, so he never got to run a single race. That's what Matt means about nobody knowing."

I jotted down "Bnnycstl—3 yr chstnt stl—grndsn Lex—no tr rec" in my notebook. "So you really have no idea what he can do, have you?" I asked.

Cobb smiled smugly. "Oh, I've clocked him once or twice. Let's just say I have a reasonable amount of confidence in him." Matt Wallens snorted impatiently and strode away, his short bowed legs giving him a rolling, nautical gait. Cobb chuckled. "Matt likes to take the dim view. That way the only time he's disappointed, something good happens."

"Not a bad way of looking at things," Tim Kanady agreed. "When you're working at the hall, it's a mighty handy thing to be able to enjoy your own misery." He slapped himself on the belly in delight at his Irish bull. "Let's see some more of these horses of yours, Cobb."

We continued down the aisle, and the proprietor of Stillwater Farm Stables showed off his string, interrupted by my questions and Kanady's jocose comments. Matt Wallens did not reappear, and I noticed that Mrs. Kanady and Eddie Terhune also seemed to have wandered off somewhere. The horses were fine-looking, well selected and well conditioned. They had obviously cost a good deal of money, and I imagined they would more than make their investment over the next few years. I told Cobb so. It pleased him.

"Of course nobody goes into racing for the money—but making

money is the way you show people you know what you're doing, isn't that right? By God, I didn't put the green in my coat-of-arms for nothing!"

When we reached the far end of the stable, Cobb said, "Well, that's the crop, Moretti. Ready to go back to the house?" I said that if he didn't mind, I'd like to wander around and talk to some of the grooms and exercise boys and perhaps find Matt Wallens again. "Suit yourself," he said. "I don't think you"ll get much out of Matt, though. Come over when you're through— we may even find a drink for you."

Cobb and Kanady headed back toward the big house, and I retraced my steps through the stable. As I passed Bonnycastle's stall, the sleek chestnut nickered and leaned his handsome head toward me. I glanced quickly around to make sure I was not under observation and then patted his withers and scratched his poll. "Sorry, friend, I still don't have anything for you," I said. "Maybe next time, if your trainer isn't around."

A few feet farther along, a short cross aisle ran from the center aisle to a side door. As I passed it I glanced toward the closed door. In a corner between it and the wall of the nearest horse stall stood Flo Kanady and Eddie Terhune, so deep in conversation that for a moment they didn't see me. Her hand lay on his arm, and from the creases in the crisp gray suiting material, I knew she was clutching tightly. Their heads were close together; she was talking in a low voice, her pretty face set in an expression of angry insistence, and he was shaking his head slowly and steadily. As I hesitated, they became aware of my presence. Mrs. Kanady dropped her hand to her side and swayed back on her heels, and Terhune straightened and half-turned toward me.

"Oh, Mr.—Morelli, is it?" she said in a lofty tone. "I'm afraid all this walking and breathing barnyard air has made me quite faint. Fortunately Mr. Terhune was here, or I might have fallen."

"Horses can be fatiguing, as I'm sure you must have found out in your career," Terhune added in what was perhaps a sardonic tone.

I offered to join Terhune in assisting Mrs. Kanady back to the big house, but they both refused. "I'm sure you have all sorts of things to do here in the stable, Mr. Morelli," Mrs. Kanady said in a tone of dismissal. "Mr. Terhune will see me safely back, thank you."

I bowed, and they preceded me along the central aisle and out the stable door. I walked slowly until they disappeared from sight. *If she was faint, it wasn't from the barnyard air,* I thought

I spent another half-hour talking with three or four stable-hands and exercise boys. They were a typical group of horse farm workers—argumentative, profane, and agreeing on nothing except the abysmal ignorance of everyone outside the horse race business—but they seemed reasonably happy in their work. Their comments on Harrison Cobb were guarded, and on Matt Wallens were grudgingly respectful, but they were enthusiastic about the horses in the Stillwater string. "Real cracks, they are," one wizened youngster insisted. "Give us five years, and we'll be the best stable on the East Coast."

"There's five money horses anyway, maybe more than that," said a freckle-faced lad with fiery red hair. "There's Napoleo, and Will's Honey, and Asmodeus, and Resolute, and Bonnycastle—he's the best of the lot!" He slapped his hand on the splintery boards beside him. "Hellfire, once the money starts coming in, we'll all be rich!"

I wrote all their names down, even though I wouldn't use any of them in my story, because I knew it would please them. Then I put my notebook away, shook hands all around, and walked back along the shaded path and through the kitchen garden to the big red brick house. Cobb's wife was no longer in the comfortable room behind the white door, but her husband, Kanady, Mrs. Kanady, and Eddie Terhune were in the same positions they had been in when I first entered the room. The three men had tumblers of whiskey beside them, and Mrs. Kanady was sipping a glass of white wine.

"Well, have you seen everything you wanted, Moretti?" Cobb asked.

"I think so, thank you. It's a fine stable you have here, Mr. Cobb. You should be making a lot of money on it in a year or two."

He chuckled. "Well, I don't plan to change our name from Stillwater Farm Stables to Poor Farm Stables. Can I offer you a drink, Moretti?"

Reluctantly I refused, explaining that I had to get back into the city and prepare my story. Mrs. Kanady looked relieved; apparently she had had little experience with social drinking in the company of newspapermen. Cobb offered me transportation to the railroad station, and a few minutes later the red-haired lad from the stable was driving me south to the Long Island Railroad station.

3

May Day in Union Square

THE ELIZABETH MEET started on schedule, and I was present to report it to a breathless world. I arrived early enough to spend an hour swapping lies with other members of the fourth estate, Sport of Kings division, while we compared the quality of the contents of our hip flasks. It was a competition in which I was unanimously acclaimed the loser.

I watched the first race from the betting ring and then walked back to the stables. One of the first faces I saw there was that of the red-haired stable boy from Stillwater Farm. He grinned as he recognized me and then immediately scowled. "Hey, you didn't put my name in the paper," he said accusingly.

"It's that damn editor of mine—he cuts out all my best things. You should have read the story before he got his hands on it."

He grinned again. "Yeah? Us lads was in it and he cut us out? The sumbitch!" He was pleased that he had approached fame so closely.

"How did your boss like the story—and your trainer, what's his name? Wallace?"

"Wallens, Matt Wallens. Oh, Mr. Cobb liked it fine. He read some of it to us—that part where you said the green in our colors stood for the money we was going to make, and about how the horses was all cracks, and the name of Stillwater Farm Stables was going to be famous all over the country. He was pleased as Punch—he joshed Matt about being a Gloomy Gus because of how Matt took it."

"Oh? Matt didn't like the story?"

The stable boy shrugged. "Matt don't like much of anything. No, he said there was plenty of time to take bows after you showed you had a reason to take bows. And anyway, what's the point of telling your business to every two-dollar horse player in the country?" He dismissed Matt Wallens's opinions with a wave of his hand. "What did you say about me in the story that the other guy cut out?"

I improvised a sentence or two about the knowledgeable and conscientious young man who labored so diligently to keep the thoroughbreds of Stillwater Farm at their peak of performance. "Jeez," he marveled. "Wait till I tell them other bozos!"

I asked him how many Stillwater Farm horses were entered in the Elizabeth meet. "We brought six of 'em over," he answered. "Their stalls are right here, in a row." We walked along the stable aisle and he pointed them out. "Will's Honey—ain't she a pretty thing? Resolute—look at that chest! Napoleo —he won the Underhill Stakes for two-year-olds at Morris Park last year. Trident—he's a real sprint horse, fastest thing you ever seen at any distance under seven furlongs. Asmodeus—his name means a devil, and a devil is what he is when he gets his blood up." He stopped abruptly and turned back toward the stable entrance.

I continued on for another step or two. "And Bonnycastle—I remember him," I said. I reached my hand into the stall. "Hello there, fellow.Want to get another good sniff of me?" The chestnut was at the back of his stall, nosing a bucket of oats. He raised his head slightly to glance in my direction, then lowered it again in a movement that expressed, more clearly than words, his lack of interest in me. "Well, if that's the way you feel—," I said.

The red-headed stable boy and I walked toward the door. "When will they be running?" I asked. He told me the days— Resolute later that day, Will's Honey on Thursday, Asmodeus on Friday, Trident and Napoleo the following week.

"How about Bonnycastle?" I asked.

He looked down and kicked a clod of dry manure. "He's running twice, once this Friday, and then again the end of next week," he said quickly. "Look, I can't talk anymore. I got to go to work."

I thanked him for his time and assured him that next time I wrote a story about Stillwater Farm Stables, it would have his name in it. "Of course, I can't promise my wretch of an editor won't cut it out," I added.

"That's all right," he said. "Good-by, Mr. Moretti." He turned and disappeared into one of the stalls, just as I heard the bugle call announcing the second race of the day.

A few minutes later I strolled through the clubhouse. Harrison Cobb was there, the center of a group that included his wife, Tim and Flo Kanady, and Eddie Terhune, among others. He waved me over and introduced me to his friends as "Fred Monk's man Moretti, who wrote that nice piece about us in *The Spirit of the Times*." Nobody offered to shake my hand. I thanked him and asked if he cared to make a prediction about his horses' chances in the Elizabeth meet. He chuckled and replied, "I think they'll make you sound like a real prophet, Moretti. You'll start finding out today—Resolute's running in the sixth race."

"I saw him a few minutes ago. He looks grand."

"Oh? You've been over to the stables today?" He took a swallow of his drink, his wide-set gray eyes regarding me over the rim of his glass. "Did you see Matt Wallens there?"

"No, one of your stable boys showed me around. All six of the Stillwater horses looked like winners to me. If I were a betting man, I think I'd take them each on the nose."

"That's why horse players die broke," Tim Kanady cried boisterously. "I thought you professional touts were smarter than that, Moretti."

"I said *if* I were a betting man, Mr. Kanady. But if I were a betting man, I wouldn't be working for a sporting paper. I couldn't afford to."

Cobb frowned at Kanady and said with mock severity, "Sounds to me as if you didn't have much faith in Stillwater Farm Stables, Tim. I take that hard, coming from an old friend like you."

"Your horses are too damn fast," Kanady retorted, a loose grin on his red face. "Never made a nickel on fast horses in my life. Slow horses, though—that's different. Slow horses and fast women, that's the ticket. Ain't it, Flo?" He slapped his wife on the hip. "Slow horses and fast women, and watch how you place your bets."

Flo Kanady glared at him and then assumed an expression of patient martyrdom. "I'm sure you'd know, my dear," she said loftily. Eddie Terhune grinned quietly and picked a bit of lint off the lapel of his hound's-tooth jacket.

Harrison Cobb and I exchanged a few more words, and then I excused myself. As I moved away from their group, I heard Flo Kanady say, quite audibly, "I know people like that have their work to do, but do they have to come into the *clubhouse* to do it?"

I went to the paddock, then back to the betting ring, where I watched the third and fourth races. I sat out the fifth with an acquaintance in the sports-writing fraternity, comparing hip flasks, and then watched the sixth from the grandstand. Resolute was one of a field of six horses in the race. He moved into place at the starting gate with confidence and economy of motion, responsive to the commands of his jockey who was conspicuous in bright new silks of purple and green. Starting odds were 5 to 1.

He didn't win, but he placed after running a very respectable race, moving up to third place at the half-mile pole and clawing his way to second place only fifty feet from the finish line. He was still closing on the front runner at the end of the race. The crowd liked him; there was a small cheer as he paraded past the judge's stand on his way off the track. He paid $4.00 and $2.80.

Well, I thought as I made notes, *Stillwater Farm Stables is off and running.*

*

The next few days were nothing out of the ordinary. I took the train to Elizabeth each morning, watched the races in the afternoon, and returned to Manhattan in the evening, where I worked for two hours transcribing my notes into comprehensible English. When I was finished at the office, I ate supper, either alone or with friends, and continued my search for a reasonable substitute for McSorley's Saloon. Once or twice, I dropped in to Zum Groben Michel, but found nothing to hold me there—neither Maisie nor Marya Perlman nor Marya's friend Sasha was in evidence, and Tough Mike, the bartender, watched my every move with deep suspicion.

On Friday two of Harrison Cobb's horses ran—Asmodeus in the third race and Bonnycastle in the seventh. Asmodeus entered the race as the second favorite in a field of nine, ran hard and well, and finished in first place to the cheers of the crowd. Two hours later, Bonnycastle, with no track record, entered the gate at 10 to 1, ran lethargically, and finished seventh in a field of eight.

The second week of the meet was marked by rising temperatures and clear blue skies and the sense that spring was gathering momentum. Buds were bursting, birds sang, ladies appeared without their cloaks and muffs and gentlemen without their overcoats. Three of Cobb's horses ran during that week. Napoleo, winner of the Underhill Stakes as a two-year-old, entered his race as the favorite and won it by six lengths, defeating two other excellent horses and paying a mere $4.20, $3.00, $2.50. Trident, who had been described by my red-headed young friend as a sprint horse, justified the description by winning a five-fur-

35

long sprint handsomely, establishing a new track record in the process. And Bonnycastle, now starting at 15 to 1 odds, ran dead last in a field of ten.

The next day was May Day. It was also the most glorious spring day so far, and one that seemed to cry out for a hiatus from mundane responsibility. I decided the Elizabeth racecourse could spare me for the first two or three races, and that I could borrow the information I needed to describe them from a co-operative colleague, subject to the usual charge of a free meal and/or a couple of drinks. I brewed myself a cup of strong tea on my gas ring and used it to wash down an otherwise unswallowable hard roll, then descended the stairs to the foyer.

Mrs. Gaugherty, my landlady, her large feet precariously positioned on the seat of an oak hall tree, was polishing the chandelier. She stopped when she saw me, put her hands on her ample hips, and regarded me from her elevated position. "Ah, Mr. Moretti, so it's off for another day at the horse races you are. Well, you've got a lovely day for it, certainly."

"So lovely it seems a shame to spend it all working for a living, Mrs. Gaugherty," I answered in the brogue she always elicited from me. "It's the kind a day a man should spend a bit of in communion with God and nature, wouldn't you say?"

She frowned and brushed a strand of gray hair from her brow. "For working people, Communion is for Sunday, Mr. Moretti," she said sternly. "Unless you're on holiday, that is. Has your employer given you a holiday, Mr. Moretti?"

"I can't say that he has, the unfeeling man," I said blithely. "An error of omission rather than commission, however, and one we should not judge him too harshly for. I'm off for a walk, Mrs. Gaugherty. Why don't you come with me? It'll put the roses of Killarney back into your cheeks."

"I've got *my* work to do, even if there are some as think *they* don't," she said with a sniff, and began polishing the brass tubing of the chandelier furiously. After a moment, she stopped and said, "I want you to be careful now. Jobs aren't easy to come by, you know. I don't know how long I could carry you if you didn't have the rent money. I've got me own bills to pay, Mr. Moretti, and with the best will in the world I'd have to show you the door in a week or two."

I smiled into her concerned face, remembering the many times she had waited a week, two weeks, and sometimes even a month for her rent from me. "I'm not going to get fired, Mrs. Gaugherty, I give you my sacred word of honor I'm not." I patted her arm. "Can I bring you anything back?"

She shook her head. "Just be careful out there. You know what day it is. The streets will be full of anarchists and communists and God knows what all. You could get yourself blown to pieces, God forbid."

I promised to look sharp and left the house. I walked to Christopher Street, then up to Waverly Place and over to Washington Square. The narrow sidewalks were more crowded than usual, and most of the people were going the same direction I was. Everybody seemed to be smiling—no doubt a reflection of the bright, brisk springtime weather which was still too unusual to be taken for granted.

I walked along the north edge of Washington Square to University Place and turned left. By now the sidewalk was so crowded I was forced to slow my pace and move at the common speed of my neighbors. We moved slowly north toward Fourteenth Street, a chattering laughing rivulet of humanity.

At Fourteenth Street the rivulet flowed into a lake. Union Square was jammed with people, and more were arriving every minute; workers with banners marched down Broadway, twenty abreast, bands playing; children ran shrieking between the legs of their elders; hucksters shouted the praises of their wares; mounted police moved carefully through the crowd, their barrel-chested horses placing their hooves as precisely as toe dancers. The police were watchful but jovial as they traded comments and jokes with the pedestrians around them. Mrs. Gaugherty's warning notwithstanding, I felt in no danger of explosive dismemberment.

I moved slowly through the crowd toward the northeast corner of Union Square, pausing to listen to one soapbox orator and then another, the first extolling the virtues of Henry George's single-tax theory, the second attacking capitalist society from the Syndicalist viewpoint. I bought a soft pretzel and ogled two shopgirls in candy-striped shirtwaists, receiving one modest demurral and one interested appraisal in reply. The Pipefitters' marching band entered the square from Broadway, playing "Hold the Fort" with more enthusiasm than artistry. At Seventeenth Street in front of Tammany Hall, I bought another pretzel and leaned against the wrought-iron railing to watch the show.

The steps of the hall seemed to be serving as the police control station. A police captain, his cap visor resplendent with the gold braid of his rank, stood halfway up the steps. His legs were spread like a sailor's balancing on a pitching deck, his arms were folded across his chest, and his head turned from side to side as he watched the movement of the crowd. Two junior officers stood behind him to carry out his orders. Every so often a civilian entering or leaving the hall would stop and speak to him, and the hauteur or obsequiousness of his response was a clear indication of his perception of the speaker's importance in the New York City Democratic organization.

One of the civilians who spoke to him was familiar. He was Tim Kanady, and from the way the captain bowed and smirked it was apparent he was held in especially high regard. Kanady paused to speak a few words into the captain's ear, and the captain assumed an expression of earnest and obedient resolution. Kanady clapped him on the shoulder and smiled, and the captain grinned in sympathetic delight. As Kanady turned to enter the hall, his eye caught mine. I nodded courteously, and he raised his eyebrows as if to indicate his inability to place me.

I turned back to the May Day carnival in Union Square. The Pipefitters had now joined the swelling throng in the square, and another band was leading another troop of workers along Broadway, this time the Amalgamated Sheet Iron Workers playing and singing "No Irish Need Apply." In the moments of relative silence between verses, I could hear yet another band behind them and, in the silences between the silences, another band behind that one.

For a few minutes I watched a pickpocket gang at work not far from where I stood. It consisted of two "stalls," a "cannon," and a "receiver," and operated with so little regard for the proximity of the police that I gathered it enjoyed a quasi-official status. The performance was expert. The gang chose only well-to-do victims, middle-aged gentlemen who had come to see how the other half lived. The two stalls, one a ten- or eleven-year-old girl and the other an attractive young woman, worked smoothly together; the girl caromed into the victim from the side, first knocking him off balance so that he stumbled into the young woman and then holding him pinned against her. As he became aware that a firm female thigh was pressed between his legs and a round young breast was somewhat flattened against his biceps, the cannon approached him from the other side and extracted his valuables so swiftly and easily that even a knowledgeable observer could scarcely believe a theft had taken place. Within five seconds the child disappeared into the crowd; the cannon passed the watch or billfold to his receiver and also disappeared; the receiver, a poorly dressed woman with a string bag, shuffled off in a different direction; the young woman accepted the victim's apology with a pretty bob of her bonneted head and modestly moved away; and the well-to-do gentleman was left somewhat less well-to-do than formerly.

I watched this "whiz mob," as the police call them, as they perpetrated three different thefts within fifty feet of the steps of Tammany Hall. As far as the captain was concerned, the pickpockets did not exist. His eyes passed over them without hesitation, without a backward glance.

After the Amalgamated Sheet Iron Workers came the Brotherhood of Meat Cutters, playing and singing "Tramp, Tramp, Tramp, the Boys Are Marching." I watched them as they pushed into the crowded square and broke ranks to mill around the various speakers, and then decided I'd had enough of the May Day rites. I began to thread my way through the crowd toward Broadway.

I hadn't gone more than a few steps when I became aware of a change in the crowd. The people around me were turning to face west, craning their necks and standing on tiptoe to get a better look at something, and I could hear a growing murmur of voices coming from that direction. After a moment I was able to distinguish words—"Whores!" "Disgusting!" "Would you believe it?" "Sense of decency—" "Drumming up business?" and "Hell of a thing!" I turned back to the Tammany steps for a better view.

Over the heads of the crowd, I saw a band of women, perhaps fifty or sixty strong, entering the square from Broadway. They were carrying banners, some of which were still being unfurled. One banner read "Prostitution Is Exploitation"; another announced "All Women Are Sisters!" As I watched, a twenty-foot-wide banner supported by three poles opened to disclose the message, "Bourgeoise Marriage Is a System of Wives in Common!—Marx."

In the front line of the marchers, under a sign that asked "Who Casts the First Stone?" was a sturdy, square-jawed woman with short blonde hair brushed carelessly to one side. Beside her, carrying herself with the hopeful defiance of the timid, was a thin young woman with boyish hips and breasts, and a clown's dot of rouge on each cheek.

The women moved into the square as the crowd drew back to give them room. Marya Perlman pushed forward to a park bench, climbed up on it, and raised her arms commandingly. "Comrades!" she called in a harsh, penetrating voice. "We are the weak, the defiled, the prostituted! Like you, we are forced to sell ourselves for bread—like you, we know the policeman's club, the belly's emptiness, the sneers and scorn of the capitalist swine and his sow! You draw back from us? Good! You make the exploiters happy! Draw back from one another too—garment-worker, draw away from steelworker! Butcher, draw away from baker! Jew, draw away from Christian! Socialist, draw away from Anarchist! Keep yourselves pure, let the capitalist pig eat you neatly, one at a time!"

A few feet away from me, the police captain was staring at the new arrivals as if he couldn't believe his eyes. The junior officers who stood behind him tugged at his sleeves, but he shook them off irritably. His lips moved as he recited inaudible prayers or blasphemies to himself. Then Tim Kanady burst through the front door of Tammany Hall, taking the steps three at a time. He seized the captain's shoulder and spun him around so violently the officer almost lost his balance. Kanady's face, as he snarled his orders, was apoplectically red. The captain listened, nodded briefly, and turned to his two assistants, who snapped to attention. A moment later they saluted and hurried down the steps and into the crowd. I saw one of them signal a mounted policeman, who trotted forward to receive his instructions.

As Marya Perlman continued to speak—and an abrasive and contumacious speaker she was—I saw the mounted police, spread out through the square, begin to draw together to form a phalanx. A thrill of apprehension ran up my spine. *Ah, there's trouble on the way and heads to be broken, or I'm a Dutchman,* I thought.

The mounted phalanx moved slowly across the square as the crowd drew back to give it room. Most of the people moved to one side or the other, but a few withdrew in front of the police, falling back to join the women gathered around Marya Perlman's bench. The mounted officers, riding shoulder to shoulder in a line a hundred feet long, stopped just short of them. One policeman in the center of the line continued forward, his big black horse shouldering men and women out of its way. He drew rein twenty feet from the bench.

"In the name of the city of New York I order you to cease and desist in this affront to public decency," he cried in a ringing voice. "Disperse!"

Marya crouched lower on her bench, as if preparing to resist a shock. "We have a right to be here!" she shouted. "This parade is authorized! Your masters, those barons who live in that castle"—her finger shot out to point to Tammany Hall— "they have authorized it! Ask them!"

Tim Kanady cupped his hands to his mouth and bellowed, "Out! Get 'em out!"

The mounted officer leaned back in his saddle. "In the name of the city of New York," he repeated.

"*We* are the city of New York, cossack!" Marya screamed.

The officer raised his arm and the line of police moved forward. They were armed with billies which were attached to their wrists by lanyards, giving them a swinging radius of a yard or more to either side. As the clubs whistled past them or cracked against their heads, the women and their allies cried out in fear and rage. Some stumbled and fell to the pavement, most struggled to keep their distance from their attackers, and a few counterattacked, stabbing at the policeman and their horses with the poles of signs and banners. I saw one woman, obviously a veteran of such encounters, dash in from the rear to jab a stick into the belly of one horse; the horse reared, almost unseating its rider. But before she could retreat to safety, his club caught her at the junction of neck and shoulder, and she disappeared from sight. Another woman caught at the bridle of a horse and was borne aloft, where she hung screaming until another billy silenced her and dropped her to the street.

All around the square, women were shrieking and men were cursing. Figures dashed to and fro, most seeking safety but some coming to join the fray. In the center of the crowd, Marya Perlman on her park bench drew herself to her full height and called in a stentorian voice, "Sisters! Brothers! Hear me!" She paused until many of the faces were turned to her and then raised her arm to point to Tammany Hall again. "See that man on the steps, comrades? The man with the fat red face of a pig, standing beside the police captain he owns? See him? It is he who sends the cossacks down on us!"

The women around her howled their fury.

"Kanady!" she continued. "Look at him! Kanady the exploiter—Kanady the pimp! How many women have you destroyed today, Kanady?" The horsemen had pushed close to her; one of them swung his club on its lanyard at her head, missing her by inches. "You will die, Kanady!" she taunted. "We, the cheated, the despised, the whores, the trash of the world, *we* will kill you, Kanady! Count the days, Kanady! Count the hours, pig!"

Another club struck her arm and she stumbled off the bench, disappearing in the crowd. A half-dozen policemen converged on the bench, their faces grim and determined as they searched for her, their horses tossing their heads with excitement.

But they didn't find her. Together with the women who had marched with her—except for the three who lay on the pavement and the fourth who wandered aimlessly in circles holding her head—she escaped the arena and found concealment among the thousands of bystanders.

For five minutes the mounted police pushed through the crowd searching for her, and then they gave it up and retired to the sidelines as the May Day carnival atmosphere reasserted itself. Hucksters reappeared in the middle of the square, a band began to play, and the whiz mob I had watched before resumed its labors. Tim Kanady spoke a few more words in the captain's ear and then disappeared within the walls of Tammany Hall.

I made some hasty notes in my notebook, mostly details such as the inscriptions on the banners and the accusatory words of Marya Perlman—not for use by *The Spirit of the Times,* but because I never knew when I might need a Sunday story to write for the *Police Gazette* in exchange for food, drink, bed, and a ten-dollar bill. I thrust the notebook in my pocket and made my way out of Union Square.

*

Two days later I returned from the Elizabeth track and entered the editorial room of *The Spirit of the Times*. It was after seven o'clock in the evening, and the cavernous room was almost deserted. Unfortunately, however, one of the few lighted desks was the one next to mine, and at it sat Bertram McAnly. He was engrossed in a copy of the *World,* his Kewpie-doll head propped up on his fat fists, his pink lips pursed in concentration.

"Good evening, Bert," I said pleasantly as I pulled my chair out and dropped into it. "What keeps you chained to your desk at this unlikely hour? Has Commodore Vanderbilt's yacht gone to Davy Jones's locker with all hands aboard?"

He shook his head. "Incredible," he said. "There's just no end to it."

"Oh, I don't know. Sooner or later we'll run out of yachts or millionaires," I said.

He looked up at me in surprise. "What in the world are you talking about, Moretti?"

I waved at the paper he was reading. "Whatever it is that's incredible, and that there's just no end to."

"Haven't you heard about the new anarchist outrage?" he demanded.

"I've been at the track all day. Nobody at the track reads newspapers. What happened?"

"A bomb! They blew up the head of the Streets and Sanitation Committee, Tim Kanady! They put a bomb in a cigar box, and it blew him to pieces when he opened it!"

I stared at him. "Tim Kanady?" I repeated. "Tim Kanady of Tammany Hall?"

"They know who did it," Bert the Barnacle went on. "Some woman who tried to organize whores into a union, if you can believe such a thing. Woman named—" He bent over the open newspaper. "—Marya Perlman, an immigrant, believed to be a Russian Jewess." He looked up, a fierce expression on his soft-boiled face. "How long are we going to put up with barbarians like that, Moretti?"

I sat down slowly and rubbed my chin. "I don't know, Bertram. Which barbarians were you thinking about?"

4

Comrades Help Each Other

ACCORDING TO THE STORY in the *World,* Tim Kanady left this vale of tears at approximately ten o'clock the previous morning, shortly after arriving at his office in Tammany Hall. A witness reported that a package had been delivered a few minutes earlier and was left upon his desk; the messenger had identified it as a box of cigars from a tobacconist whose name the police did not at this time care to reveal. It was assumed that Kanady had opened the box and thus accomplished his own removal, which was accompanied by great destruction within his office, but fortunately little outside.

The writer or his informant must have been present at Union Square on May Day, because his description of Marya Perlman's threat of vengeance tallied exactly with the words I had jotted down in my notebook.

The story ended with the assurance by the authorities that the suspected assassin would be apprehended within twenty-four hours.

When I finished reading the story, Bert the Barnacle wanted to continue airing his sense of outrage, but I pleaded the need to work on my Elizabeth report. After a few minutes he turned off his light and bustled indignantly out. I waited until I was sure he was gone and then threw down my pencil and leaned back in my chair. *Saints protect us,* I thought, *my drinking companion has blown up a sachem of Tammany Hall. If I don't get back into McSorley's soon, I may find myself having a glass with the future assassin of President Benjamin Harrison.*

I tried to get back to work, but my mind kept straying to Zum Groben Michel and Union Square, to the passionate anger and raffish wit of Marya Perlman, to the dedication of her friend Sasha and the despair of the woman named Maisie. I helped myself to a swallow or two from my flask, but it did nothing to improve my concentration. Finally I called it a day.

My rooms on Bleeker Street lay almost a mile north of *The Spirit of the Times*'s offices on Chambers Street in the shadow of City Hall. It was a dark night and chilly, so I caught an electric car on Broadway. Both sides of the street were lined with office buildings and warehouses consecrated to the wholesale dry goods trade, and most were dark at this hour. The lighted windows of occasional restaurants and saloons shone through the darkness like the fires of castaways hoping for rescue, and the rare pedestrian glimpsed under a street light seemed exposed and vulnerable.

The car rattled north to Bleeker Street, where I descended and walked to my building. The foyer was lit, and the chandelier gleamed with soft yellow highlights. I checked the letterboxes on the wall—my compartment was labeled "Moretti, second, front" —and found nothing. I glanced at myself in the hall-tree mirror and had no particular reaction. I climbed the stairs, entered my room, closed the door behind me, and reached out to turn up the gas. And froze.

Marya Perlman sat on my dilapidated sofa and looked at me with an expression compounded of caution and expectancy. Her short legs were crossed like a man's— one ankle on the opposite knee—and one arm lay along the back of the sofa, exposing a small circle of perspiration in the armpit. Her bosom rose and fell with her breathing. Her eyes glittered under her heavy brows.

"Hello, my fighter against male tyranny," she said in a low, throaty voice. "Up the rebels! Have you read the paper today?"

"Up the rebels," I answered through dry lips. "As a matter of fact, I have. A fascinating affair, surely. Give me your side of it, and I'm sure we'll both make a pretty penny from Fox at the *Police Gazette*. Exclusive story on what drove you to commit the crime of the decade, brutal facts about the life of the dispossessed and downtrodden—"

She halted me with a raised hand. "Enough. You think I blew up that Tammany swine with a cigar-box bomb?"

"Well, didn't you? Oh, I understand your reasons—I was in Union Square on May Day, and I saw what happened. I watched Kanady give the order that started the whole thing—"

As I spoke, she shook her head deliberately. "No, no, no. It was not I. Believe me. For an *attentat* I might choose a governor, or even perhaps a mayor, if he was famous enough—but the head of the Streets and Sanitation Committee? *Oy gevult!*" She studied my face. "You believe me, Moretti? I do not lie, you know."

I nodded slowly. "Yes, I believe you," I said to my own surprise. "I don't know how many other people will, though. The story I read in the *World* doesn't leave much doubt what the authorities think. I'd say they already have you tried, convicted, and sentenced."

"That is true. And there is even more they will use against me—what they haven't told the newspapers yet." She brushed her short hair to one side and squared her jaw truculently. "The cigar box—it came from a shop in the building where I live. The tobacconist is a comrade, a well-known anarchist. He and I have been— close."

I went to the window and drew the curtains. Then I produced my flask and made us two short drinks. I handed Marya one and sat down on the sofa beside her. "If you had sent the bomb, or if this tobacconist had sent it on your orders, would the messenger have mentioned the name of the cigar store?" I asked thoughtfully. "As far as I'm concerned, it works the other way around—the fact that he mentioned the store at all makes it look like a frame-up. By the way, how did you find out which store the box came from? The papers didn't mention it."

"The police have already been there. Johann Beimeyer is in custody. I heard it from a comrade this afternoon. I was at Sach's Cafe on Suffolk Street, and they came there too. I barely got out the back door in time." She threw the whiskey down her throat as if it were vodka. "Prosit!" She set the glass down on the floor and folded her hands behind her head. "So, Paddy Moretti. The cossacks search for me at my home, at the cafes where I eat, at the places where I work. They jail my friends or follow them like bloodhounds. I am a fugitive, unable to visit any persons or places I have been connected with in the past. Where can I go, *gospodin?* Where can I find shelter from this relentless pursuit?"

"At Paddy Moretti's?"

"At the Greenwich Village apartment of my friend the racing reporter for *The Spirit of the Times,* whose path has crossed mine but once in my life!" she continued triumphantly. "No one can possibly connect us, Moretti! We live in different worlds — one time only they intersected at Zum Groben Michel, and no one there ever heard of your name!" She put her warm hand on mine and squeezed. "I will be safe here, no matter how they try to destroy me!"

This is impossible, I thought. *Why am I acting as if it isn't?* I looked at Marya's hand, red, rough, with the nails bitten to the quick, and thought about the warmth and firmness of her grasp. "Yes, I think you will," I said, "if you stay in the apartment and don't make any noise. There's a landlady on the first floor, but she never pokes around."

Marya released my hand. "It's settled then!" she cried happily. Her eyes sparkled as she took my face between her hands. "We will be good comrades here, Moretti! We shall help each other, as good comrades do!"

She pulled my head down and raised her mouth to mine. Her lips were soft, pliant, and very alive. She kissed me deeply and thoroughly for a considerable length of time. When she drew her head back, the blood was pounding in my temples like timpani.

"Comrades help each other," she repeated in a whisper, her breath hot on my cheek. She took my hand and pressed it against her firm breast; I could feel the nipple rising against my palm. Her eyelids lowered sleepily and she moistened her lips with the tip of her pink tongue. "Ah, Moretti, *lyubenyu,*" she sighed, "help me."

"Oh, I will, I will!" I answered hoarsely. I kissed her again and felt her fingers on my chest as she began to unbutton my shirt. We moved slowly into the bedroom, leaving a trail of garments across the floor. When we arrived at the bed, there were no more clothes to drop.

Marya Perlman made love slowly and fiercely and with total concentration. She was completely in charge, controlling each movement, setting the pace, heightening sensation. I felt like a novice in the hands of a master. When my moment of ecstatic release arrived, fully half an hour after our arrival in bed, I collapsed on the damp sheet, feeling as boneless as Pheidippides after his run from Marathon.

Marya propped herself on an elbow and looked at me affectionately. "Ha, Moretti, we are good comrades to one another, are we not?"

"God, yes!" I breathed.

"That's good." She put one hand lightly on my thigh, causing me to shudder involuntarily. "And comrades help each other."

"And it's very helpful we've been, for a fact," I agreed.

"Now you must help me again, *gospodin.* No, not that way— I mean you must help me to stay out of the hands of the police.

I will not be captured and tried and convicted of a crime I did not commit. I need help to prove my innocence, or else to leave town safely. You must go to my uncle and explain to him."

I raised my face from the pillow. "Your uncle? You want me to go to your uncle?" She nodded. "All right," I agreed. "Who is he? Where do I find him?"

"At the place where you work—at *The Spirit of the Times*. You mentioned him yourself, when we were talking at Zum Groben Michel."

A cold worm of dread began to uncoil in my stomach. "He works on the paper with me? And I mentioned him to you at Mike's? You don't mean—you can't mean—" I couldn't bring myself to finish the sentence.

Marya did it for me. As her warm hand moved caressingly on my thigh, she said, "I mean your editor, Otto Hochmuth. He is my Uncle Otto."

*

The next morning I brewed a pot of tea and brought Marya a cup. She sat up in bed, and the bedclothes fell away to reveal her superbly full breasts. She yawned and stretched, arching her back like a cat. Then she took the cup from my hands and inhaled the steamy aroma. "Ah, you spoil me with your attentions, Moretti," she said archly. "How will I ever return to the proletarian world after you serve me breakfast in bed?"

I bent to kiss her in a proprietary manner. "Comrades help each other," I said.

"Do you leave now to see my uncle?"

I nodded. "That I do. And to tell you the truth, it's not the conversation I've looked forward to with the most anticipation in my life."

"Don't worry. He is my Uncle Otto, and he will not abandon me to the cossacks." She paused and then added. "He is a *schmok*—but he is my uncle too."

I cautioned her not to make any more noise than she could

help and left the apartment. Outside the sun was bright and the air was fresh, and I decided to walk to work. My thoughts kept alternating between the night just past and the morning just ahead, between the glowing face of Marya Perlman and the jaundiced complexion of her Uncle Otto. My spirits moved in wave motion, cresting in the recollection of certain gasps and groans and sighs (*You didn't acquit yourself too badly on the Field of Venus, me boyo*) and plunging into the troughs as I anticipated Hochmuth's reaction to the message I bore (*You know what tyrants do to the messengers who bring them bad news, don't you?*). Involved as I was in these abrupt transitions from euphoria to despair, I reached the newspaper office almost before I knew it.

I was glad to see I was not the last staff member to arrive. Bert the Barnacle's desk was, gratifyingly, still empty. Hochmuth's, of course, was not. He was at his desk, a pencil in one hand and a sheet of copy paper in the other. His green eyeshade sat foursquare on his bony forehead. In the morning sunlight, his face had the color and texture of Braunschweiger.

I could see no advantage in delay. I crossed the room and stopped in front of him. "A beautiful spring day it is, to be sure, Mr. Hochmuth," I said.

He did not look up. "From the singing lilt of the Emerald Isle in the voice, I believe I recognize Mr. Moretti. What brings you here at this almost indecently early hour?"

"Well, I wondered if we could have a little talk, Mr. Hochmuth." I paused. When he didn't answer, I added, "It's personal, you might say."

"Oh?" He still didn't look up. "What kind of personal? Gambled-your-money-away-and-can't-pay-the-rent personal? Barred-from-the-track-and-can't-write-your-story personal?"

"To tell you the honest truth, it's not a *me*-personal thing at all, Mr. Hochmuth. It's a *you*-personal thing. What I mean is, you're the person that it's personal about."

He raised his eyes to mine. "Succinctly put, but unclear," he said. "Are you saying you wish to talk to me about a matter

relating to my personal life as opposed to my professional duties?"
I nodded dumbly. "I was not aware our relationship included this
area, Mr. Moretti."

"It's about your niece, Marya Perlman," I blurted. "She
needs help, and she says you're the only one who can help her."

For a few moments he sat without speaking or changing his
expression. Then he pursed his lips, drew gently on his right
ear lobe with his fingers, and said quietly, "How do you know
about my niece, Moretti?"

I explained that I had met her three weeks before, and during
our conversation had mentioned that I worked for *The Spirit
of the Times;* that I had seen her again from a distance at the
May Day disturbance in Union Square, but had not spoken to
her; and that she had appeared in my rooms the night before
with her request that I help her to reach her uncle.

"She's at your place now, I take it?" he asked. I assented.
"Where she spent the night, of course," he continued. I didn't
answer. "And she intends to stay there for the time being?"

"She has nowhere else to go," I said.

"I see." He picked up his pencil and sheet of copy paper.
"Though it may have escaped your attention, we are in the
process of producing a newspaper here, Mr. Moretti. However,
I am in the habit of taking my luncheon in City Hall Square,
and I would be glad to continue this conversation at that time."

"Yes, sir."

"Third bench from Broadway, facing south. Twelve-thirty to
one. And you better bring something to eat—I'm afraid I only
have sufficient food for myself."

*

When I approached Hochmuth's bench, the first thing I saw
was two hundred pigeons. They were surging around his high-
buttoned shoes in a transport of greed as he tore the crusts from
his sandwich and sprinkled the crumbs among them. The expression on his face was almost sympathetic until he saw me.

53

The pigeons glared as I forced my way among them and sat down on the bench. "Lovely weather for a spot of lunch al fresco, Mr. Hochmuth," I said as I unfolded the sheet of newsprint that contained my meatball sandwich.

Hochmuth dispensed a final handful of largess and then leaned back on the bench and regarded me. "I didn't ask you to join me here for a meteorological discussion," he said shortly. "The subject is my niece. I want you to tell me everything you know about her involvement in this anarchist outrage."

"The first thing to tell is that I don't believe she *is* involved in it," I answered. "She says she isn't, and I believe her. I don't think she'd deny murdering the pope himself if she'd done it."

His sour expression lightened momentarily. "No, I don't think she would either. Well." He took a bite of his crustless sandwich and chewed it thoughtfully. "If she didn't do it, then someone else did," he continued. "Some other anarchist maniac, I assume."

"Perhaps," I said neutrally. "In any case, it's herself the police are after, and herself they'll try to convict."

He nodded. His expression changed from sourness to sadness. After a moment he began speaking in a toneless voice. "I've never been able to help my niece, and I doubt if I will be able to now. When she came to this country I offered her a home with me. I've never married, and I thought it would be comfortable for both of us. I was wrong. She informed me I was a bourgeois exploiter, a tool of the capitalist class, and she would make her home with her elder sister in Rochester and join the proletariat in the garment factories." He looked at his sandwich as if he had forgotten what to do with it. "Her sister wrote me when Marya was married, and again when she was divorced, and again when she moved here to the city. I sent her a letter at the address I had for her. Perhaps it was the wrong address; at any rate, it was never answered. The next I heard of her was when she blew up —when the police *say* she blew up a Tammany Hall assemblyman."

As he talked I chewed my meatball sandwich and the dill

54

pickle that had come with it. When he lapsed into silence, I said, "She told me she needed help to prove her innocence or to leave town. That's why she asked me to come to you."

Hochmuth turned to me with a glint of anger in his eyes. "As a fellow employee of *The Spirit of the Times,* Mr. Moretti, I'm sure you'll understand that my salary has not allowed me to put by large sums of money for the use of ungrateful nieces who wish to elude the constabulary. You may report to her that if she thinks she'll get any money out of me," he said slowly and distinctly, "she has another think coming."

"I'll tell her that," I said.

"However," he continued, "there is one thing." His mouth pursed to the size of a buttonhole. "As I recall, you've enjoyed a certain success, quite unconnected with your journalistic talents or the lack of same, in the solution of crimes of violence. There was an affair in Saratoga Springs four or five years ago, if memory serves, and then another out in Kansas or Iowa or one of those places. Therefore, if you would care to address yourself to the problem of establishing the innocence of Marya Perlman—"

"You'll give me a leave of absence from the paper?" I interrupted.

"—while at the same time continuing your duties on the newspaper," he continued, "I should have no objection." Primly he opened his sandwich to disclose its filling, an orderly row of sardines, and began to eat them one by one, holding each by the tail as he lowered it into his mouth.

"It's all right with you," I rephrased, "if I singlehandedly clear your niece's name, as long as I put in a full ten hours of coolie labor here on Chambers Street first."

He didn't answer until he had swallowed the last sardine. Then he said, "Or afterwards, whichever you prefer." He began shredding the two now naked slices of bread. The pigeons, sensing a resumption of their feast, hurled themselves against our shoes. He cast a handful of crumbs to the assembled multitude.

I said, "Very well, Mr. Hochmuth, I'll do what I can, which

55

may very well be nothing at all." I rose to my feet and looked at him with what I hoped was well-concealed loathing. "I'll keep you abreast of my efforts."

"But not on company time, I trust," he answered drily. As I kicked my way through the pigeons, he called after me, "Mr. Moretti, if you leave for Elizabeth immediately, I doubt if you will miss more than the first two races. No doubt you will be able to get the necessary facts on them from one of your colleagues."

"Good day, Mr. Hochmuth," I said, because I could think of absolutely nothing else to say.

He was incorrect: By the time I got to the track the first three races were over. I spent half an hour finding out what had occurred in them and then went to the clubhouse to watch the fourth race. Harrison Cobb was there, talking with a man whose back was turned to me. Cobb was wearing a loud tweed suit and smoking a long cigar which he used to emphasize and punctuate his remarks. I waited until he appeared to have reached the end of a thought and then approached him. "Good afternoon, Mr. Cobb," I said. "I've been meaning to congratulate you."

Cobb stared at me a second without recognition, and his companion turned toward me with a frown. I realized that the second man was The Owner—the august Frederick Follinsbee Monk III, publisher of *The Spirit of the Times*. "And a good afternoon to you, Mr. Monk," I added.

"Ahh, it's your man Moretti—it *is* Moretti, isn't it?" Cobb asked. "Or is it Morelli, or Moroni, or Macaroni? Something like that, I'm sure." He sounded in high spirits.

Monk nodded curtly. "Good afternoon, Moretti." He hesitated, and then said grudgingly, "Not a bad piece you did about Cobb's stable. Been meaning to send you a note about it." The Owner had a head as bald and red as a tomato two days short of full ripeness; his expression, even when offering compliments, was petulant, as though they were being extorted from him.

"With the success you've been having, it looks like *veni, vidi, vici* is the perfect motto for Stillwater Farm Stables," I said ingratiatingly.

"You're right, we've been lucky the first time out." Cobb tugged on his lapels and blew cigar smoke complacently. "Will's Honey may just be the fastest little filly on the East Coast. Trident's greased lightning in sprint races, and Asmodeus and Napoleo are born champions. And Resolute's not a bad horse— maybe not a stakes winner, but he'll always run well in his class. Don't you agree, Monk?"

The Owner grunted. "I've seen worse horses from older stables, Cobb. *Lucky* is the word I would have chosen, too."

"Oh, there may be a bit more to it than luck," said Cobb with a chuckle. "Admit it, Fred—there's been some pretty shrewd judging of horseflesh involved here. As a matter of fact, you wouldn't mind having a piece of Stillwater yourself, would you?"

Monk's eyelids narrowed, and his expression changed from irritation to anger. He withdrew a cigar case from his pocket and deliberately selected a Havana *claro*. He clipped it and lit it before replying. "There are many things I wouldn't mind having, Harrison," he said coldly. "Part of a stable is one of them, as I think I told you once. Not the only one, but one of them." The two men regarded one another in silence, and I felt a current of emotion between them that made me uneasy.

Cobb's grin became wider. "Well, you just cross your fingers, Fred, and maybe some of that luck will fall your way." He blew a smoke ring. "Or maybe it won't."

I spoke to break the growing tension. "How about Bonnycastle, Mr. Cobb? What do you expect from him?"

He tapped the ash off his cigar, and his smile disappeared. "Bonnycastle may be my first mistake. I don't mind telling you, Moretti, he hasn't lived up to my expectations. I'm very disappointed. You've seen him run, of course?"

I said I had, twice.

"Once second to last, the other time dead last," Cobb continued glumly. "And he's a grandson of Lexington— or that's what they told me, anyway." He shook his head. "I don't understand it. Matt Wallens says he's a plater and we might as well get rid of him."

Frederick Follinsbee Monk III made a noise that might have been a snort of amusement. I asked Cobb, "Are you going to?"

He sighed. "I've got him entered in a race at Gravesend the first day of the meet, and I guess I'll give him one more chance. If he doesn't do better there, they can send him to the glue factory for all of me."

The bugle called the fourth race and the horses filed onto the field. Behind us someone called, "Cobb! What about it, Cobb? Who do you like?" Cobb turned to wave and then said to me, "Now, if you'll excuse me, Moretti—"

"Certainly," I said. Then, as an afterthought, I added, "Oh, Mr. Cobb, may I express my sympathy."

He frowned. "What for?"

"The shocking death of your friend Mr. Kanady. I'm sure it must be a grief to you, the two of you being so close and all."

"Close? How do you mean, close?" He stared at me with hard eyes. "What makes you think we were close?"

"Why, just that I saw him with you at Stillwater Farm Stables, and then here again at the track. I wondered if the two of you might be partners."

"That's an interesting question, isn't it?" The Owner asked in a mocking tone. I saw he was smiling slightly as he drew on his cigar.

"Partner? Kanady?" Cobb asked.

"In the stable. I thought he might have an interest in your stable."

"No," he said abruptly, and then, as if remembering his manners, he added, "You're right, it was a terrible thing. Ghastly. Makes you wonder how long we'll keep tolerating this kind of violence in America. I'm sure they'll catch the woman, and I hope they hang her. Pardon me." He nodded curtly and turned his broad back on me. The Owner regarded me a moment longer before he also turned away.

I watched the race and made my notes and then started out of the clubhouse. Since I intended to visit the stables, I picked up a few sugar cubes from one of the tables and dropped them into my pocket.

Approaching the stalls occupied by the horses from Stillwater Farm Stables, I looked for a familiar face, but saw no one I recognized, neither Matt Wallens nor the red-haired stable boy nor any of his colleagues. The first of Cobb's stalls was occupied by Will's Honey, the filly. I called her name and offered her a sugar cube. She sniffed it fastidiously before taking it, and after she swallowed it, she withdrew to the back of her stall, as if to say she wasn't the kind of lady to be seduced by a taste of sweets.

Next came the barrel-chested Resolute and the imperial Napoleo, both of whom condescended to accept a cube as long as it didn't commit them to anything. Trident acted as if he could take it or leave it alone—but just the same he took it. Asmodeus eyed my hand with more interest than the sugar, making me so nervous that I almost dropped the cube to the floor when he bared his great teeth. He chose the sugar, however, perhaps on the theory that he could get the hand on the next bite.

Bonnycastle was in the rear of his stall with his head in the corner. I called him twice and rapped my knuckles on the gate before he turned to look at me. "Here, boy, here, Bonnycastle," I called softly, extending my hand toward him. "Nice, sweet sugar, old fellow. Maybe it will make you run a little better."

He tossed his head and pawed the floor idly. I continued to call him. After half a minute or so, he moved away from the wall and took a few steps toward me. His eyes inspected me with little interest. I jiggled the sugar cube and repeated, "Here, boy, here, Bonnycastle." Slowly he came close enough to sniff the sugar, and I felt his warm breath on my palm. He opened his mouth and took the cube. In the few moments before he retreated to the back of his stall again, his head was no more than two feet from my own.

Isn't that a remarkable thing? I asked myself. *When I first saw him on Long Island, there was a wen the size of a dime at the corner of his right eye. I wonder where it went?*

"What the hell do you think you're doing? Who told you you could come in here?" rasped an angry voice at my elbow. I turned to look into the face of Matt Wallens.

"Sure, and it's me job, Mr. Wallens," I said placatingly. "I'm Moretti, of *The Spirit of the Times,* remember? I had the pleasure of writing that extremely complimentary article about Stillwater Stables."

"I remember. Didn't they teach you not to go sneaking around barns without permission? Now get out of here—I don't have time to talk to you."

"I'm just leaving," I said placatingly. "Congratulations on an auspicious beginning for the purple and green—with the sad exception of poor Bonnycastle, that is." I put on a sympathetic expression, "Hardly what anyone expected, is it?"

"Anybody who expects anything in this business is riding for a fall, mister. Now, out!"

I left the stable and returned to the grandstand.

Four hours later, I was back in Manhattan at my desk in the office of *The Spirit of the Times.* Bert the Barnacle was blessedly absent, and I wrote my report on the day's racing quickly, without interruption. When I had finished, I glanced around the big room, now almost completely empty. At a desk near the far wall sat Clem Harber, our baseball writer and general trouble-shooter. He was leaning back in his chair with his feet on the desk and his eyes closed; except for the regular mastication of his jaws he seemed totally inert. As I crossed the room toward him, he turned his head toward a nearby spittoon and let fly without opening his eyes. He missed by six inches.

"Good try, Clem, but no cigar," I said.

He opened one eye. "They're making the gobboons smaller these days," he said in his nasal voice. "Hello, Moretti. What do you want from me?"

"Oh, nothing, nothing at all. A bit of pleasant conversation, a touch of companionship at the end of a busy day——"

"I don't keep a bottle in my desk, you know," he said, closing his eye.

"As if that would be of any importance to me whatever," I said with a chuckle. I sat down on the edge of his desk. "Tell me something, Clem. In your capacity as connoisseur of the fleshpots, have you ever heard the name of Tim Kanady bruited about in the Tenderloin?"

He opened both eyes. "Tim Kanady?" he repeated. "The recently atomized Tammany Hall sachem?" I nodded in affirmation. "His name is — or was, I should say—not entirely unknown in the demimonde," he continued. "In particular, he was rumored to have a piece of a notch palace called the Circus. Why?"

"This Circus—I've heard it mentioned before. What kind of place is it?"

"I've never been there, Moretti. I understand it specializes in the kind of unusual activities I've never been in the market for. I'm a religious fellow, and I like my diversions to be of the Adam-and-Eve, David-and-Bathsheba persuasion. I'm not attracted by whips, small boys, or domestic animals."

"And you think Tim Kanady was one of the owners?"

He shrugged. "I don't think anything. What I said was, he was *rumored* to be. By the way, did you hear about the lecherous landlord? He was fined for spreading roomers. Don't bother to laugh if it's a strain." He spat at the cuspidor again and very nearly hit it.

"Was Kanady supposed to be involved in any other places, Clem? Or any other kinds of businesses?"

He thought a moment and shook his head. "Not that I remember hearing about. That doesn't mean anything, though. I'm not really an authority. Now what's the story, Moretti? What are you working on?"

"Where's the Circus located, Clem?"

He frowned in irritation. "It's in Chelsea, in an old brick mansion on Eighteenth Street between Eighth and Ninth. And that's the last goddamned word you're going to get from me until you tell me why you want to know."

I clapped him on the ankle in a comradely manner. "You've been a prince, Clem. When the time comes for explanations, you'll be the first to know." He cursed me matter-of-factly and closed his eyes, his jaws chomping as methodically as a metronome.

*

I caught the Broadway car and got off at Bleeker Street. There was a saloon on the corner where I bought slices of cheese and salami, a loaf of bread, and an onion. As I stepped out onto the street again, it occurred to me that I might very possibly end this escapade being charged by the police with harboring a fugitive from justice. I peered nervously into every face I passed on my way home. None of them seemed to belong to a detective, however, nor did I see any suspicious figures lurking in the shadows near my door.

Marya Perlman was lying on the sofa with her hands crossed on her bosom and her eyes closed. She was breathing slowly and deeply. I closed the door behind me and quietly bent over her. "Wake up, macushla," I whispered. "I've got supper for you if you've got a kiss for me."

Her eyes opened and she looked up at me sternly. "I am not asleep. I am renewing my psychic energy," she said. "Sexual activity is depleting to the psyche, just as it is to the physical constitution. You should also renew yourself, comrade. Lie down on the floor and think of an empty blue sky."

Feeling slightly miffed, I retorted, "The only empty thing I can think of is me own belly. You can renew yourself all you want. I'm going to eat a sandwich." I unwrapped the food and put it on the table. "Salami, strong rat cheese, an onion to take the top of your head off, fresh, crusty bread—and somewhere around here I've got a jar of mustard—" Behind me I heard the sofa springs creak as Marya sat up.

"Of course physical renewal is also important," I heard her say. "Proletarians must keep strong if they expect to triumph over capitalist tyranny." She moved to my side and picked up a slice of salami. She sniffed and said approvingly, "Ah, much garlic. Good!"

"Best way I know of keeping us proletarians strong," I said, as I reached for the mustard jar.

5

My Introduction
to the Circus

AFTER WE FINISHED EATING, Marya demanded an account of my meeting with her uncle. As I repeated his words, her brow darkened. "He said that?" she interrupted. "He said, if she thinks she will get money from me she has another think coming?"

"I'm afraid so."

"And I said he was not a *schmok*. I must learn not to sentimentalize the bourgeoisie. They are invariably worse than I give them credit for." She scowled and brushed her short hair back from her temple. "Very well. No help from Uncle Otto —good! We still have you, comrade!"

I wrapped up the remaining half loaf of bread in a sheet of newspaper and set it on a shelf. "That's true, for what it's worth. It just may not be worth very much."

"Bah. You said Uncle Otto mentioned two murder cases you solved. You are a detective, *gospodin*. You will find the assassin of Kanady and turn him over to the police and clear my name of this ridiculous charge."

"I'm not a detective, Marya. I'm a racing reporter of mixed breed who's barred from McSorley's. It's a frail reed you've picked to lean on."

"No. Not a frail reed. A stout oak rod." She patted my knee. "Remember, comrades help each other, Moretti."

The combination of her touch and the words sent my thoughts in an amorous direction. I put my arm around her shoulders. "I've just had one of my most helpful thoughts," I said.

Her elbow struck my stomach like a pitched baseball. "We have not yet renewed our psychic energies. Please do not act irresponsibly. We must consider the problem of locating the true assassin."

I took my arm away and touched my solar plexus gingerly. "I don't suppose you'd believe me if I told you my psychic energies are filled to the brim and slopping over? No, I don't guess you would." I got up and found my whiskey flask. "Renew your alcohol level?" She frowned and shook her head. I splashed two fingers into a water glass and sat down in my shabby armchair. "All right, let's consider the problem. When you were in Union Square threatening Tim Kanady, you called him an exploiter of women, a pimp. Was that because he owned a share of the Circus?"

"Of course. A man named Axel Klepp is the proprietor, but Kanady was one of the backers. It is well known to everyone but the newspapers."

"Well known to the police? Well known to Tammany Hall?"

"Certainly—to them best of all."

"How do you know?"

She sighed and explained carefully, as if to a backward child, "The women who marched with me to the square, many of them work at the Circus. You remember the woman at Zum Groben Michel's, the one you bought whiskey for?"

"Maisie?"

"Maisie Goertz, yes. She works there now. She went there when she was too sick to work on the street any more. Now she services rich pigs—I would not tell you how. It was Maisie who told me first about Kanady. She said he came often, and the other women told her it was important to please him because he was an owner. She said he wanted—terrible things, and she was afraid not to do them. Ah, Moretti, I think I am sorry I *didn't* kill that filthy *momser!"*

"Now don't be dwelling on that thought." I sipped my drink. "So Kanady lost his temper when he saw a bunch of who — of *filles de joie* from his own establishment marching in the May Day parade, and sent the police down on them to teach them a lesson. Causing your perfectly natural reaction of making a speech and putting your head into a noose."

She frowned at me impatiently. "Come, Moretti. How are you going to locate the assassin?"

I emptied my glass and rose from my armchair. "I'm going to exercise my sleuthlike instincts while you stay here and renew your psychic energies. Conjure up that empty blue sky, comrade."

"Where are you going, Moretti?"

"The Circus," I answered. I gave her what I hoped was a devil-may-care smile and closed the door behind me.

*

As I walked past the three-story brick building that housed the Circus, I listened for sounds of revelry, but Eighteenth Street was as quiet as a country churchyard. Behind every window the curtains were drawn, allowing only an occasional sliver of light to be seen from the sidewalk outside. From Eighth Avenue behind me to Ninth Avenue a hundred yards ahead, the street was deserted.

I continued a few steps past the building and then crossed the street and headed back toward the lights on the corner of Eighth Avenue. A sign hanging over the sidewalk read "THE FIGHTING COCK." I pushed open the door and entered.

The saloon was small and dark and smelled of uncollected garbage as well as beer. Three men leaned against the bar, and one of the tables was occupied by two women and a tiny man with a pouter-pigeon chest and a humped back. I put my foot on the bar rail and smiled at the bartender, a sour-faced fellow with a handlebar mustache and a strawberry birthmark under his ear. "Draw me a bumper of your best, and have another to keep me company," I cried cheerfully. He filled a fishbowl stein for me and a small glass for himself. "Ten cents," he said. I gave him a quarter and left the change on the bar. He drank off his beer, gave me a long impassive look, and walking down the bar, took up a position facing the other customers.

I studied my neighobors surreptitiously as I drank my beer. Two of the men at the bar were workmen, dressed in dungarees and heavy shoes. The third was a slight man with overlong hair and a weak chin, wearing an excellent tweed suit. The workmen were drinking beer, the other man whiskey. From the corner of my eye I inspected the three persons at the table. The two women wore the sealskin sacques that were almost a uniform in their profession. The fatter one sported a feather boa around her shoulders, rather the worse for wear, and her slender sister toyed with a rope of imitation pearls. The hunchback, whose feet dangled three inches above the floor, wore a well-cut gray suit and matching spats. He held a long cigar between two beringed fingers and toyed with a cocktail glass on the table in front of him.

I chose the slight man in the expensive tweeds. Picking up my fishbowl and sidling down the bar, I said, "Well, sir, you've a glass there that wants refilling, and I'd consider it an honor to have it refilled for you." I signaled the bartender and then put out my hand. "Paddy Moretti's me name, sir, and a bit of sociable conversation is my desire."

He took my hand as if he didn't know how to avoid it and gave it a perfunctory pump. "Bobbitt, Mr. Moretti, Willis Bobbitt," he said in a reedy voice. "I don't know about another drink. It's getting late, and I was just getting ready to leave."

"I won't hear of it!" I said, waving the bartender to fill up the man's glass. "If there's anything I hate, it's drinking alone. A vicious habit—it's my belief it's responsible for all of the ills associated with alcohol. When a man raises the glass of fellowship, the drink's no more harmful than mother's milk; but when he drinks alone, it's liable to rot his liver and steal away his brain. Why, I know a gentleman who's all of eighty-eight years old, and he's had a sociable pint of whiskey every day of his life for the past seventy-one years—"

I continued this foolishness for a few minutes while I had Bobbitt's glass filled twice more. Then, when I judged him to be sufficiently off guard, I nudged him companionably and asked, "Where are you headed when you leave here, Willis? Down the street to the Circus?"

"What?" he asked in alarm.

"The Circus, man—don't pretend to me you never heard of it! Why, I figured you for a regular when I first clapped my eyes on you! That's why I wanted to have a sociable chat with you!" I drew closer to him and dropped my voice. "I've had me an itch to visit the Circus ever since I first heard about it, but I don't know if they'd let me in—not unless I had a regular to vouch for me."

"I don't know what you're talking about," Bobbitt said. He pulled out an Irish linen handkerchief with embroidered initials on it and wiped the back of his neck. "I just happened to stop here for a drink."

I winked. "Sure you did, Willis. Don't worry. Say, is it true that you can watch girls doing it with a dog? Saints preserve us, but wouldn't that be something to see!"

Behind me I heard a pair of shoes hit the floor. The hunchback had left his chair and was walking toward the door. He moved with a curious crablike motion, his left shoulder pushed forward and his right foot dragging behind. He didn't speak, and no one spoke to him. When the door closed behind him, there was a moment of silence. Then the two women at the table began a spirited dialogue, and the bartender moved toward me and picked up my beer stein. "About time for one on the house," he said grimly.

"Don't forget me friend Willis," I cried. "And yourself, of course, my good boniface!"

He set our refilled glasses before us and swallowed half his small beer. I laid a fifty-cent piece on the bar and leaned close to him. "I bet there's plenty you've seen, with your saloon here only a stone's throw from the place. You'd be knowing most of the regulars by name, I wouldn't be surprised."

He put the half-dollar away under his stained apron. "From the Circus? Yeah, I guess I know one or two of them." He looked at me expressionlessly, waiting for my next question.

I clapped Willis Bobbitt on the shoulder to include him in the conversation. "Did you know me old friend Tim Kanady, the assemblyman? God rest his soul, it was himself that told me about the Circus, and all the unusual entertainment it offers."

Willis Bobbitt emptied his glass hurriedly and said, "Thank you for the drinks, Mr.—ah, I really have to go now. Excuse me." I reached out my arm again, but he ducked under it and hurried toward the door. A moment later he had disappeared.

The bartender watched his exit and then turned back to me. "Kanady, you say? Tim Kanady?" He wrinkled his brow in an unconvincing expression of perplexity. "A little skinny fellow with a toothbrush mustache, is he? No, wait a minute—that's Tim Kerrigan." He thought again, and then called, "Hey, Pearl, you ever hear of a fellow named Tim Kanady? Goes to the Circus a lot?"

"*Used to* go to the Circus," I corrected. "Tim's gone to his heavenly reward, the unlucky man."

The two women at the table inspected me with interest, and the fat one with the fur boa said, "Tim Kanady? Seems to me I've heard that name before. Come over here and buy us a drink and I'll try to remember."

"That's right, you go sit with them, friend," the bartender said. "Pearl and Annie, they're real good at conversation. I'll bring your drinks over."

I sat down in the chair recently vacated by the hunchback. "Ah, ladies, this is a pleasure! Conversation with two beautiful women, spiced by the cup that cheers—what more could a man ask?" I leaned back to let the bartender set my fishbowl in front of me and place fresh glasses before the two women. "And you said you knew my friend Tim Kanady? Then I have to envy him, dead man though he is."

The woman with the rope of pearls drank half her cocktail. Her companion regarded me speculatively. "I didn't say I knew him, honey. I said I'd try to remember if I did." She put a puffy hand on mine. "Don't be in such a hurry, love. Drink your beer. The night is young." She sipped her cocktail with exaggerated delicacy, her small, pouched eyes watching me carefully.

"Nothing could suit me more," I replied, swallowing beer.

The bartender said something to the two workmen. They scooped up their change and went out the street door.

"You said your friend's dead?" the woman called Pearl asked. "That's too bad. What happened to him?"

"You probably read about it in the papers. A terrible anarchist outrage it was. The dear man was blown up by a bomb in his own office—"

The street door opened again. Two men entered. One was the hunchback, a look of malevolent satisfaction on his face. The other was a man of my height, wearing a yellow and black checked suit. He had sleepy eyes, coarse black hair over a low forehead, and very broad shoulders.

"That's him, he's still here!" the hunchback cried, pointing to me. Behind the bar the bartender gave a sigh, and the two women relaxed in their chairs. "Hello, Sharkey," said the fat one. "We kept him here. His name's Paddy Moretti. He was asking questions about Tim Kanady."

Sharkey and the hunchback came straight to the table. Sharkey said, "Get up. Mr. Klepp wants to see you."

"That's all very well, but do I want to see Mr. Klepp?" I replied. "Get yourself a drink and we can discuss it."

My hand was lying on the table, palm down. Sharkey placed his fist upon it. He was wearing brass knuckles, which he rocked back and forth twice. I felt as though every bone in my hand broke. The pain was so unexpected and intense that I gasped aloud.

"I said get up. Mr. Klepp wants to see you," Sharkey repeated.

I rose to my feet. "There's no call to get violent," I said through gritted teeth. "I was planning a visit to the Circus a bit later anyway." I massaged my hand carefully and bowed to the two women. "Ladies, the minutes I've spent with you passed like hours."

Sharkey gripped my arm just above the elbow, and we walked toward the door. I waved to the bartender. Sharkey opened the door with his free hand. I noticed he was still wearing the brass knuckles.

We walked diagonally across the deserted street to an areaway which ran along the side of the building that housed the Circus. Sharkey turned me into it. Thirty feet back was a heavy oak door. He opened it with a key and pushed me inside. "Up the stairs," he ordered. I preceded him up a narrow spiral staircase to the second floor. As I hesitated he struck me sharply in the back with the brass knuckles. "Keep going up," he snapped. Obediently I climbed the next flight of steps, which led to a short, uncarpeted corridor. At the end of the corridor was a door, painted white. "Inside," said Sharkey. I opened the door.

The room beyond was furnished as an office. Behind a black and red lacquered Chinese Chippendale desk sat a man wearing a funereal black suit which made his pale complexion seem absolutely colorless, as coldly white as the surface of the moon. One of his eyelids drooped, as if he were permanently winking. It was impossible to estimate his age—he could have been anything from thirty-five to sixty-five.

"Yes?" he inquired in a soft, melodious voice.

"It's him, Mr. Klepp, the one that was asking questions," Sharkey said.

"You're interested in my establishment, are you? May I ask why?"

Before I could answer, Sharkey intervened. "They said he was also asking about Tim Kanady."

Klepp's pale blond eyebrows rose. "Well, you are a curious man, Mr.—?" He waited while his auditory question mark faded into the silence.

I hesitated a moment before answering, not sure whether to give my real name or not. Before I could decide, Sharkey said, "He said his name was Paddy Moretti."

"That's correct. Paddy Moretti at your service," I said with a bow of my head.

Axel Klepp frowned. "Moretti—Paddy Moretti. Don't I know that name?" He began to move papers around on his desk and gave a grunt of satisfaction as he raised a copy of *The Spirit of the Times* in the air. "Of course—the eminent racing correspondent of my favorite sporting paper. This is a pleasure, Mr. Moretti—I'm a great devotee of the Sport of Kings, and your dispatches add considerably to my enjoyment of it. I was reading your account of last week's Elizabeth meet only this evening." He dropped the newspaper on his desk and put out his hand without rising. I stepped forward to shake it. It was cold and slightly damp.

He leaned back in his chair. "Now then—what brings you to a deadfall like The Fighting Cock, asking questions about the Circus and Tim Kanady? Isn't that a little far removed from your usual beat, Mr. Moretti?"

"That it is, Mr. Klepp, that it is. But to tell you the truth I've heard tell of the Circus for months now, and some of the things I've heard sparked my curiosity, you might say." I would have stopped there, but I sensed that my explanation was inadequate. "So when I heard a rumor the other day that Tim Kanady had his money in the place, I thought I'd like to find out about it."

"But I don't understand," Klepp said in his softly resonant voice. "You write about horse races. Tim Kanady was an assemblyman down at the Wigwam. The Circus is an establishment devoted to the exotic in entertainment. I don't see how these facts have any reference to each other."

72

"You're saying that Tim Kanady had no interest in the Circus?" I asked.

He looked pained. "I'm not saying anything at all, Mr. Moretti. I'm asking why a sporting reporter is sniffing around a whorehouse and asking questions about a murdered politician. You answer my question and then we'll see about answering yours."

"Why, it's just as I told you, Mr. Klepp," I protested. "I picked up a rumor, and had me a hunch, and thought I might spend a few hours scratching that itch of curiosity we reporters suffer from." I smiled disarmingly. "There's nothing more to it than that, I give you my oath."

I heard Sharkey shift his weight behind me. He must have communicated some signal to his employer, because Axel Klepp shook his head almost imperceptibly.

"Now listen to me, Mr. Moretti," he said softly. "There is only one kind of relations I enjoy with the press, and that's no relations at all. It disturbs me to have a reporter asking questions about my establishment. It disturbs me, and I won't have it. Many newspapermen are welcome here as customers—you'd be surprised how many, and how important they are—but they leave their professional duties outside. Otherwise—"

"Otherwise?" I repeated.

"Otherwise, I'm afraid I should have them hurt. I don't make threats often, or idly, but I want you to understand me clearly. If, after you left here tonight, I were to conclude that you were continuing to snoop in my affairs, I would have no choice but to have you crippled for life."

I swallowed.

His long, pale fingers massaged each other. "Is that perfectly clear, Mr. Moretti?" I said it was crystalline. "Good. We understand one another. May I offer you some brandy? Or perhaps you'd enjoy an exhibition downstairs? We have one beginning"—he pulled a gold watch from his pocket—"in fourteen minutes exactly."

"Thank you kindly, but I have someone very special back at my rooms—someone I've already kept waiting too long," I said like an utter fool.

"Oh?" He smiled slightly. "Then I won't urge you to stay. It's been nice meeting you, sir. Take my advice and stick to the job you do so well. Show Mr. Moretti out the way he came in, please, Mr. Sharkey."

Sharkey touched my arm. "Yes, sir." We left the office and descended the spiral staircase to the ground floor. He held open the oak door that led to the areaway and followed me as I walked toward the street. Just before I emerged from the deep shadow beside the building, his hand clamped onto my arm and pulled me to a halt. I felt the hard edge of the brass knuckles as he pressed them against my top vertebra. "What he said—remember it," he breathed into my ear. Then he drew his fist back slightly and shot it forward again. The crack in my ears was like the Day of Judgment, and pinwheels of fire exploded behind my eyes. I stumbled forward and almost fell to my knees, barely regaining my balance before I sprawled in the gutter.

After a few seconds the stunning pain moderated to a throbbing ache. Sharkey was gone; I was alone on Eighteenth Street. Holding my head, I walked unsteadily toward the lights of Eighth Avenue, which drew closer very slowly. I passed The Fighting Cock on the other side of the street.

There's no doubt about it, I thought, *tomorrow I really must pay a visit to Uncle Paolo.*

6

A Family Visit
and a
Consolation Call

IT WAS ALMOST MIDNIGHT when I got back to my rooms.
Marya was asleep on the couch with a blanket over her. I started
to walk quietly past her toward my bedroom, but she heard me
and sat up. "Have you found out anything?" she asked.

I told her I had found out that Axel Klepp didn't like publicity, and that being hit on the head with brass knuckles causes
headaches.

"They hit you? The *schwein*! Was it because of the questions
you asked? You made them nervous, perhaps?" she demanded.

I found my flask and took two fingers without benefit of glassware. "Ahhh. I don't think so. I think it's reflex action, any time
they decide anyone's sniffing around the Circus. If I had made
them nervous, I don't expect I'd be home now. Or ever."

She considered my comment judiciously and nodded. "I think
you are right. I think this Klepp is a true monster, capable of
any viciousness. Maisie told me he asked her to bring her little
sister to work there. In the exhibitions. A ten-year-old girl."

I took another drink and offered the flask to Marya. She shook her head with an expression of distaste, so I screwed the cap back on. "That's terrible," I said. "The kid didn't go, I hope."

Marya shrugged. "Not this time. Bunny is still living in her family's flat on Hester Street. But next time, who knows? After she has been hungry and sick a few more times." Her eyes flashed at me. "Would you presume to judge her?"

"Not for the world." I closed my eyes and pressed my fingers gently against my eyeballs, hoping it would ease the throbbing ache behind them.

"Come here," Marya ordered. I knelt down in front of her as she directed, and she placed her hands on my cheeks with the tips of her fingers pressed against my temples. "Close your eyes, *liebchen*," she said gently. Her fingers moved in a circular pattern, and as I began to relax, I felt as if I were afloat and rising and falling with the waves. After a timeless interval, I heard her voice ask, as though from a great distance, "Is that better now?"

I opened my eyes and found my headache was almost gone. "I think so—yes, it is, much better." I looked up at her. "It's a ministering angel you are, Marya Perlman. Let me have those healing hands of yours." I began kissing her stubby fingers. She jerked her hands away, and her face flushed in embarrassment.

"*Mashuggah!*" she said. She leaned back on the couch and pulled the blanket up to her chin. I moved off my knees onto the couch beside her.

"You've made a new man of me—my psychic energies are bubbling up like beer from a bunghole," I said emotionally. I put one arm around her shoulders and attempted to pull down the blanket with the other. "Comrades help each other," I reminded her.

"Moretti—stop!" she ordered. When I didn't immediately obey, she struck at my solar plexus again. Fortunately this time the blow was cushioned by the blanket, but it was still forceful enough to knock most of the wind out of me. "I mean it,

Moretti!" she said. "This is not the time for healthy sexual expression!"

"It isn't?"

"Your psychic energies may be restored, but your physical resources are at a low ebb. What you need now, *gospodin*, is sleep. Go to bed."

I protested vehemently, but my protests were to no avail. Five minutes later Marya was breathing regularly on the couch, and I was in my bed trying to put the memory of her firm warm body out of my mind.

I awoke to find the room bright with sunlight and Marya beside the bed with a cup of tea in her hand. "How do you feel?" she asked as she handed it to me.

I inventoried myself as I tasted the dark, steaming tea, which was much stronger than I make for myself. "Everything seems in working order," I said. "Physical and psychic energies fully restored. The only thing that hurts is me stomach, bedad."

"Good," she said with an approving nod. "The sun is high— it is time to continue your investigations. Get dressed. I will close the door." She marched purposefully from the room, pulling the door to behind her.

When I had completed my ablutions and dressed I joined her for a second cup of tea and a slice of bread smeared with jam. As I ate I studied her face, square-jawed and purposeful, her clear, wide-spaced eyes, so dark a blue they sometimes seemed black, her heavy brows and short, tousled hair. *This is a woman, Moretti,* I thought. *Maybe more of a woman than you've ever known.*

"Where do you go today?" Marya asked.

"Gravesend—their spring meet opens today. But before that I have to pay a visit to Mulberry Bend."

Her eyebrows rose. "Mulberry Bend? But that is in Little Italy. Why do you wish to go there?"

"I want to see my Uncle Paolo."

"See your uncle?" she repeated. "Why would you take time for family visits now, while the bloodhounds bay outside, and a murderer walks the streets?"

"It has to do with not wanting to be crippled for life," I answered.

She frowned uncomprehendingly. I checked my pockets for notebook, pencils, handkerchief, and wallet, then walked to the door. "I'll bring home some good food tonight—maybe some good news too, if I'm lucky. Meanwhile, remember Mrs. Gaugherty downstairs." She nodded silently and I left the flat.

My Uncle Paolo lived on Mulberry Street, just below the bend that marks the center of the old Five Points neighborhood. His apartment was on the second floor of a tenement; the first floor was taken up by *il Negozio Moretti,* the food market he owned. I paused at the door to savor the blended aromas of garlic, fish, Chianti, oregano, onions, peppers, gorgonzola, and slightly over-ripe fruit. My cousin-in-law, Ettore Magnutti, was behind the counter chopping up eels. He glanced up, recognized me, and said sourly, "It's you, is it?"

"Buon giorno, Ettore. Come sta?" I asked cheerfully. "How's Teresa? How are the kids?" Teresa was Uncle Paolo's daughter.

Ettore shrugged his broad shoulders and began a fresh eel. "All right. Luisa has been sick all winter. It costs a lot of money."

I told him I was sorry for his problems, which was not particularly true. He grunted and finished the eel. "What brings you down to the slums?" he asked. "Going to write an article about us criminal Italians?"

"I want to see Uncle Paolo. Is he back in his office?"

"He was ten minutes ago." He swept the chopping block clear with his knife and slapped another eel down. "Knock before you go in."

"Sure, and don't I always, me boyo?" I said in my heaviest brogue, hoping to annoy him. He didn't answer. I walked back through the store to the closed door at the rear and knocked on it.

"Avanti, per favore," called Uncle Paolo in his flutelike voice.

Paolo Moretti, my father's elder brother, was a slight, fastidious-ly dressed man with white hair worn *en brosse* and a white mustache that curled around both sides of his thin-lipped mouth. He wore a diamond ring that was reputed to have cost over five thousand dollars. His silk shirts were monogrammed, and I had always suspected his underwear was, too. Chief Inspector Byrnes of the New York City Police Department believed he was a god-father in *la società Mafia,* and Chief Inspector Byrnes was right.

He extended his hand to me and I bowed over it. "Ah, Patrizio, you do your uncle the honor of a visit this year," he said drily. "*Grazie!* I am overcome with gratitude!"

"I have been intending to visit you these last two months, *Zio Paolo,* and only the unimaginable pressure of my duties has pre-vented me," I said.

"No doubt." He gestured toward a chair. "Sit down, sit down. Have you heard from your father lately?"

I told him all the news I had of the Morettis of Goshen, Ohio, which was very little. He listened carefully and asked questions about my father and my brothers and sisters, but not about my mother, whom he blamed for causing my father to settle in the Midwest, and for being Irish. After we had exhausted the subject, he leaned toward me and put his fingertips together. "*Buono!* Now, Patrizio, what is the reason you have chosen to visit your old uncle today?"

"I need help, Uncle Paolo. There is a man who has threatened to have me crippled if I continue my investigation of him, and it is necessary for me to continue that investigation. Therefore I need protection."

"I see. And who is this man who threatens you?"

"His name is Axel Klepp. He runs a bordello called the Circus."

He nodded. "I have heard of him. A flesh merchant. He has no connection with us. He belongs to the *forestieri*—the outsiders. Why do you wish to investigate him, Patrizio?"

I explained how I believed the reason for Tim Kanady's death might be found in his connection with the Circus and with Klepp. He frowned. "But was he not killed by the woman, the anarchist with the bomb? This is what the newspaper says." I said I didn't believe so. The woman had told me she was innocent, and I believed her.

Uncle Paolo studied me with a hint of amusement in his eyes. "So, you believed her. Perhaps because she was lying down when she said it, eh? You are not afraid of a bomb under the bed, Patrizio?"

I felt my cheeks grow hot. "She's an honest woman. If she had killed Kanady she would have told the world about it. That would have been the whole point. It would have been an *attentat*, an open political act, not a murder."

"Ah, *mio nipote*, how have you become involved with these people? If you would come to see *la famiglia* more often, if you would attend your church—" He sighed and shrugged his well-tailored shoulders. "Ah, well. We cannot allow a Moretti to be crippled by an outsider, no matter how foolish he is. My brother would never forgive me." He rose from his chair and rapped sharply on a door in the back wall. "Hey, Tomaso! Gaetano! *Avanti!*" Almost immediately the door opened, and two men entered. I had known both of them for years, but they looked at me without any sign of recognition.

"*Si, Don Paolo?*" asked Tomaso, a tall, middle-aged Sicilian with half of his right ear missing.

Uncle Paolo gave them their orders. Until he gave them instructions to the contrary, they were to follow me during the daytime and take turns watching my flat during the night. They were to stay far enough away from me to remain inconspicuous, but close enough to render assistance if needed. They were not to hurt anyone unless absolutely necessary, and they were under no conditions to be apprehended by the police. Were there any questions?

"No, Don Paolo," said Gaetano, a small, slender man whose swarthy complexion gave evidence of his Gypsy blood.

"One question, Don Paolo," said Tomaso. "The *lupara*—should I carry it?"

The *lupara* is a sawed-off double-barreled shotgun with a hinged butt and a hook that allows it to be hung inside a man's overcoat. I awaited Uncle Paolo's answer with considerable curiosity.

He thought a moment and then nodded. "This Klepp, he is a dangerous man, I have heard. We cannot take chances with our Patrizio. Yes, take your *lupara*. But do not use it unless there is no alternative. And do not be taken with it."

Uncle Paolo excused them, telling them to wait on the street for me. After they had gone, he smiled at me benignly. "It is my pleasure to be of assistance to you, *mio nipote*. I have always believed the greatest joy of being one of the *prominenti* is to do favors for friends and family—and to be rewarded by their favors in return."

"I too value that joy," I said.

"A week from Saturday is the birthday of my wife's cousin's daughter Giuseppina. She will be eighteen, and we are having a small dinner in her honor. My wife thinks it is time for her to meet young men. I would be delighted to welcome you to my home on that occasion. At six o'clock *essato*."

I bowed. "I look forward to it with the greatest anticipation, *Zio* Paolo."

He reached out his hand in dismissal. "Let me know when you no longer need Tomaso and Gaetano. *Arrivederci*, Patrizio."

I walked back through the store, thinking that among the Morettis nothing comes free. The only mental picture I could conjure up of Giuseppina Angeletto was six or seven years out-of-date; she was wearing a starched white confirmation dress and standing with one foot on top of the other, giggling. She was skinny, sallow, and seemed to have more teeth than she could close her mouth over. I sighed in resignation. Ettore Magnutti was now cleaning fish behind the counter, eviscerating and decapitating them with machinelike efficiency. I waved my hand

and said, *"Ciao, paesano."* He didn't bother to answer.

Outside, Mulberry Street was aswarm with all the varied specimens of humanity that juxtapose themselves in a neighborhood with a density of 1,100 persons to an acre. I elbowed my way among grandmothers with shopping bags, mothers holding babies, gang members ogling all women between twelve and forty, beggars playing violins, pushcart peddlers shouting their wares, organ grinders, prostitutes beckoning from first-floor windows, drunks in doorways, pickpockets, and an occasional honest workman on his tardy way to work. Once or twice I glanced over my shoulder, but Tomaso and Gaetano were invisible in the jostling crowd.

It was good to know they were there.

I made my way toward City Hall. Inside, I set myself the job of finding Tim Kanady's home address. The custodian of the City Directory was able to inform me that it was on Beekman, not ten minutes' walk away. Since it was not yet eleven o'clock, I decided to visit it before setting out for my day's duties at Gravesend.

As I approached the stone steps in front of the Kanady brownstone, the front door opened and a man appeared. He took one step out onto the porch, then turned and spoke to someone inside the house. A pair of white arms wrapped themselves around his neck. He moved back toward the doorway, and a female body in a dressing gown moved out to join him. They kissed briefly but intensely, and the man withdrew himself from the embrace and the woman closed the door.

I waited until the man descended the steps and hailed a passing hack. I recognized him; he was Eddie Terhune, the rising legal light of Tammany Hall.

I climbed the steps and knocked on the door. For thirty seconds nothing happened, so I knocked again. At length the door opened, revealing a tired-looking middle-aged woman in a maid's uniform. "Yes?" she asked. She looked Irish, so I replied with a touch of the brogue.

"Would ye be so kind as to announce me to your mistress, me dear? It's Paddy Moretti of *The Spirit of the Times* calling."

She looked at me sternly. "She's not here— come back some other time." She began to close the door. I blocked it with my shoe.

"Then it's remarkable how fast you got into your uniform," I said.

She hesitated. "What do you mean?"

"Seeing as how not two minutes ago you were kissing your boy friend good-by in a silk dressing gown. It must have been you, mustn't it, if your mistress isn't home?"

"What? Me kissing a boy friend?" She stared at me incredulously. "Are ye loony? Get your foot out of that door before I call the police!"

"It's all right, Maggie, I'll talk to the man," said a carefully genteel voice I recognized. Flo Kanady appeared in the doorway. She was still wearing the white silk dressing gown. "All right, Mr. Moretti. I'm not aware that you have any claim on my time—but what do you want?"

"A few moments of conversation, Mrs. Kanady, nothing else. A question or two, and then I'll be off."

She stepped aside and held the door open. The maid snorted in disapproval and disappeared into the back of the house. Mrs. Kanady gestured toward the sitting room. "We'll go in there," she said, leading the way. It was a prim, uncomfortable room. She sat down on the front edge of an oyster-gray satin chair and looked at me coldly. I waited a moment for her invitation to seat myself, and when it was not forthcoming, eased into a tufted oak armchair.

"It's sorry I am about your loss, Mrs. Kanady," I began.

She raised one hand. "Please spare me both your sympathy and your accent, Mr. Moretti. You didn't know Tim well enough for the sympathy, and I've heard you speak without the accent. Now what do you want to see me about?"

I looked at her carefully. I remembered my impression when I had met her at Harrison Cobb's Long Island Home— of an Irish colleen prettiness thrown out of balance by too much powder and rouge. I saw I had done her an injustice. She was a beautiful woman with dark auburn hair, gray eyes, and a clear, luminous complexion. Her lips were thinner than they might have been and bracketed by lines of bad temper, but her nose and chin were almost classic, and her neck was long and gracefully curved. Beneath her dressing gown, her bosom swelled provocatively.

"I want to talk about your husband, Mrs. Kanady. I'm looking into the circumstances of his death."

"Is that why you were watching my house?" she asked contemptuously. "My husband was murdered by a crazy anarchist woman, blown up by a bomb. Everybody knows that."

"And why did she kill him?"

"Because she held him responsible for sending the police down on her in Union Square, when she led a troop of prostitutes in the May Day march. Don't you read the newspapers, Mr. Moretti?"

"Yes, ma'am, but I don't always take them for Holy Writ. The question I'm really interested in is why your husband was so upset to see prostitutes marching in a parade. Was he that high-moraled a man?"

She looked at me in silence a moment. She raised her chin and ran one finger down her throat. "Are you here to try to blackmail me?"

"Not a bit. Believe me. Also, I should say I haven't been watching your house. I simply happened to be outside when your friend left this morning."

"Whom you recognized, of course?" I bowed my head in assent. She hesitated a moment, then leaned back into her chair and crossed her legs. "Oh, the hell with it," she said. "It would have come out sooner or later anyway. Only this *is* a little early for the grieving widow to be caught consoling herself. Eddie won't like it at all." She looked sharply at me. "Are you sure you want to do this, Moretti? Eddie Terhune is a bad man to have for an enemy."

84

"You don't understand, Mrs. Kanady. I'm not going to sell a story to the *Police Gazette,* and I'm not trying to blackmail you, and I don't give a tinker's damn who you console yourself with. The only thing I care about is who killed Tim Kanady."

"That woman did."

"I don't think so. So let me ask you again: why was your husband so upset to see prostitutes marching in a parade?"

She waved her hand impatiently. "Because they were *his* prostitutes, you fool. They worked for him at a filthy den he owned an interest in."

"The Circus?"

"You know about that? Yes, the Circus. Tim invested some money with a man named Klepp two or three years ago. I found out about it by accident last year, and Tim admitted it. He thought it was funny. *Funny!* Tim Kanady wasn't the nicest man in New York, Moretti."

"Neither is Axel Klepp." I thought a moment. "If Klepp and your husband were partners, then Klepp stands to take over your husband's interest now. Unless Kanady made some arrangement with him to let *you* inherit it. Did he?"

"Of course not. He knew I wouldn't touch that filthy business with tongs." She spoke forcefully, but her eyes were suddenly thoughtful.

You didn't use tongs to pick up the money it brought in, I thought. *How much went into your fine clothes and fancy furniture?* Aloud I said, "Just as a matter of curiosity, does Eddie Terhune know about Kanady's connection with the Circus?"

"No —why would he? You don't think I'd brag about it, do you?"

"No, but Kanady might. You said he laughed about it. And both of them worked together at Tammany Hall."

She drew herself up with the hauteur she had shown during our earlier meetings. "Please understand this, Mr. Moretti. Mr. Terhune is a gentleman, as unlike my late husband as it is possible for a man to be. He is refined in his tastes and modest in his

85

speech, and avoids vulgarity like the plague. The very idea of him listening to the boorish confidences of my husband is laughable."

"It's odd that two such different men would both be friends of Harrison Cobb," I said.

She shrugged. "I don't see why. They were both prominent men, and both extremely interested in horse racing. Naturally they both knew Cobb."

"Is Terhune that interested in horse racing?" I asked. "Somehow I had the impression he didn't care much one way or the other."

"Oh, no. Mr. Terhune is *very* interested. He knows bloodlines and track records and all those things. If he could afford it, there's nothing he would rather do than own some race horses himself."

"I know how he feels, Mrs. Kanady. I've been bit by the same bug myself." I could see by her expression that she considered an enthusiasm which was fitting and proper in her cavalier to be common and coarse in me. I changed the subject. "Would you try and think of anyone who might have profited by your husband's death, Mrs. Kanady? Or who hated him enough to want him dead?"

"The papers say he was killed by that anarchist woman," she said stubbornly.

"Putting that aside for a moment, can you think of anyone else with a motive?"

Her mouth twisted in a bitter smile. "In general, anyone who has ever gotten to know and love him. Specifically, nobody. And now I think that's all the time I can give you, Mr. Moretti. Please take your wild goose chase somewhere else." She rose from her chair and stood waiting.

I stood up and thanked her for her time. "And please be assured, ma'am, that I have absolutely no interest in your private affairs," I added.

"For your sake, I hope that's true," she said coldly.

I bowed and turned toward the door. At that moment I heard steps in the front hallway, and then a strong masculine voice called, "Maggie, I went off without my valise—have you seen it?" Eddie Terhune appeared in the doorway. His eyes widened as he saw Flo Kanady and me. "Hello," he said, "another admirer, Flo?" He ran his eyes over me from shoes to haircut. "They do say a cat may look at a king, so I guess it can look at a queen too. Even a Kilkenny cat."

"Hello, Mr. Terhune," I said. "I was just offering my sympathies to Mrs. Kanady, and the subject of one of his business ventures came up. An establishment called the Circus. I wonder if you've ever heard of it?"

"No, should I have?" He turned from me to Flo Kanady, and there was an edge of anger in his voice as he said, "You know you need your rest—I'm surprised to see you wasting your energy talking to newspaper reporters."

Flo lowered her eyes and answered in a small voice, "You're right. I think I'll go lie down for a few minutes. Excuse me, Mr. Moretti." She looked at me with what might have been a bit of apology in her eyes and left the room. Terhune and I stood in silence, listening to her footsteps ascending the stairs. Then he said, "I think I want to know what brought you here today."

"I had a question or two about Mr. Kanady's business connections, as I said."

"For what reason? Why do you come here bothering Mrs. Kanady about business? What are you up to?" He settled one hip on a mahogany reading table and swung his foot in the air. His sharp-featured handsome face wore an expression of suspicion. "Since Mrs. Kanady's recent bereavement I have helped to shield her from annoyances, which is the category in which I must place you, Moretti, unless you can tell me exactly what you want to know and why you want to know it."

I looked into his clever eyes and sighed. "It's not all that easy to do, Mr. Terhune. I'm following a will-of-the-wisp. I asked myself the question, if an anarchist didn't kill Tim Kanady, then who did? And if there's any answer to that, it surely involves another question, which is, *why* did he do it?"

Terhune stared at me in surprise a moment before he threw back his head and gave a yip of laughter. "And if pigs had wings they could fly, if pigs *wanted* to fly! Why for one moment should you think that the anarchist Perlman woman didn't kill Kanady? She promised she would in front of a hundred witnesses!"

"But *if*—just for the sake of argument, say—*if* she didn't, then who would have had reason to?" I waved one hand to indicate helplessness. "I said it was a will-of-the-wisp."

"And this is what you're bothering Mrs. Kanady about? I think you better stick with horse racing, Moretti, and leave detecting to the professionals. You just don't have the flair for it."

He indicated the door, and I took a step toward it. Then I hesitated and said, "Of course, if an anarchist *did* kill Kanady for political reasons, I'm not sure the other sachems at Tammany Hall should be feeling too safe." I don't know why I said it, except to annoy Terhune.

His face paled, either from anger or fear. "Get out, Moretti," he said. "Get out and don't come back."

I walked down the hall to the street door. A clock on the wall showed 11:45. I let myself out of the house and trotted down the steps. It was time to go to Gravesend.

7

Reflecting Upon the
Luck of the Irish

THE FIRST OF THE THREE Long Island tracks to open is Gravesend, which is located in Brooklyn. Because its opening day signifies the arrival of the long-awaited vernal season to every horse player in New York, and because it is the closest and most convenient of the three tracks to reach, its opening-day festivities are extremely popular. When I arrived shortly before the second race, the stands and the clubhouse were jammed.

As I pushed my way through the crowd near the betting ring I saw Edderly, the *Tribune*'s racing columnist. Since I was on better terms with him than almost any of my other friendly competitors, I tacked to port and allowed the crowd's pressure to push me to him.

"I'll bet you a drink you can't tell me what happened in the first race," I said in greeting.

"Damn you, Moretti, does Hochmuth know his racing department depends on the compassion of his competitors? The contemptuously condescending compassion of his competitors, I should say?"

I produced my flask from my hip pocket and offered it to him. He swallowed four times before he handed it back, noticeably

89

lighter. "Alice's Beau takes an early lead—at the quarter mile post it's Alice's Beau, Centurion, and Topsy—in the backstretch Alice's Beau is dropping back—Topsy and Centurion are neck and neck and here comes Ali Baba—they're coming out of the far turn into the homestretch and it's Centurion, Topsy, and Ali Baba—now they're heading for the wire and it's Centurion, Ali Baba, and Topsy—and Windjammer wins by a nose!"

I looked up from my notebook. "Windjammer?"

"He came up out of nowhere. Nobody even knew he was in the race. A real thriller. Please be grateful enough to hand me that flask again."

I shook my head firmly. "A contract is a contract. I wouldn't want to weaken a man's respect for the pledged word."

Edderly regarded me sorrowfully from red-rimmed eyes. He was a big, soft man with thinning hair and a long receding chin. His clothes were threadbare, unpressed, and none too clean. The redness in his eyes was more likely to have come from sleeplessness than dissipation—I happened to know his wife was an invalid and his daughter suffered from chronic respiratory trouble.

"When you die may you have an undrunk bottle of whiskey in your pocket, Moretti," he said.

"Maybe we can have another taste later," I called over my shoulder as I headed into the crowd again. *Racing reporters should never get married,* I told myself. A sudden chill of loneliness ran through my veins.

At the betting ring I checked the entries in the upcoming races. Bonnycastle was entered in the fifth race, one of a field of eight. The odds were 30 to 1. I stared at the figures thoughtfully.

One of the bookmakers, a scholarly looking fellow in a celluloid collar whose name was Cronin, approached. "It's your lucky day, Moretti," he said. "If I've ever seen a man with winner written all over his face, it's you. Just put your money here and tell me who it's on, so I can get a bit down for myself." He held out his hand.

I hesitated. I almost never bet on a race, both as a matter of principle and because when I do I hardly ever win. However, if I had ever been sure of anything in horse racing, it was that Bonnycastle would win this race. Everything argued in favor of it: the fact that the horse I had seen at Elizabeth was not the same horse I had seen at Stillwater Stables Farm; the fact that Bonnycastle began this year with no track record; and the fact that the horse running as Bonnycastle had lost disastrously in his previous outings at Elizabeth. In his first race, "Bonnycastle" had started at 10-to-1 odds and finished seventh in a field of eight; in his second, the odds had fallen to 15 to 1, and he finished dead last. Now, with the closing of the Elizabeth track and the transporting of the horses to Gravesend, it was the perfect time to substitute the real Bonnycastle—with the wen at the corner of his right eye—for the bogus one. When the grandson of Lexington won against a field of platers, he would return sixty dollars for every two-dollar bet.

"Come on, Moretti," Cronin urged. "You've got the luck of the Irish with you today. You know you do. Now who's it going to be?"

Even though my experience has shown me that the luck of the Irish is mostly bad, I dug my bankroll out of my pocket and counted it. My total assets were $23.84. I handed a ten-dollar bill to Cronin. My indecision must have shown on my face, because he kept his hand extended to me. After a brief hesitation, I placed the two five-dollar bills on top of the ten.

"Twenty dollars on Bonnycastle— on the nose," I said.

His eyes widened. "Bonnycastle? In the fifth?" he asked incredulously.

"I believe that's what I said," I said negligently, inspecting my fingernails.

"It's your money," he said as he scrawled out a marker. As I accepted it and stuffed it in my pocket, he studied me. "All right, Moretti, what do you know?" he asked in a hoarse whisper. "You can tell me. I won't ruin it, I give you my word. I'll just cover myself with a dollar or two. What's the story?"

"Just what you said, Cronin. The luck of the Irish. Look in a mirror—maybe you have it written there too." I gave him a wave and strolled away from the betting ring.

I was in the grip of conflicting emotions. The dark side of my nature told me I had placed at hazard more than five-sixths of my worldly assets, or at least that part of them that was represented by cash, and went on to remind me that my track record on wagering was not one to inspire confidence. The bright side pointed out that impeccable reasoning predicted a six-hundred-dollar windfall. It expressed itself, as usual, in Irish symbolism. *The little green man's sitting on the pot of gold, and you're got him hanging by his heels*, it exulted.

I made my way through the crowd listening to one voice and then the other. Once a third voice made itself heard, asking whether, if I believed there was a plot to cheat the betting public, I should not take action to prevent it. That voice, however, was immediately drowned by the other two.

I found myself in front of the main stables and entered. The first person I saw inside was my friend the red-haired stable boy, who gave me a friendly grin. The second person, unfortunately, was Matt Wallens, whose brow darkened as he recognized me. He stepped toward me swiftly in a rolling, bandy-legged gait. "All right, mister, out!" he rasped. "I'll not have my horses disturbed before a race!"

Suddeny I remembered where I had seen Matt Wallens before. It had been at Monmouth Park in the early eighties, and his name hadn't been Wallens then, it had been Warhull. "Sailor" Warhull, he had been called, not because he had ever been to sea, but because of his bowlegged walk. He had been involved in a horse-doping ring, and my old friend Hugh Llewellyn—known to his friends as Taffy the Welshman—had gotten the goods on him. As I remembered, Warhull had given evidence against his fellow felons and had won a suspended sentence while they went to jail. He had, of course, been barred from all the major tracks as a consequence.

And now Warhull was working for Stillwater Farm Stables, and Stillwater Farm Stables owned the putative Bonnycastle. Another piece of supporting evidence for my hypothesis clicked into place. I smiled as I looked the scowling trainer in the eye. "Of course, Mr.—Wallens, was it?" I said lightly. "Somehow I have trouble remembering your name. It seems like it should be something else. I'll wish you good luck on the race today. May everything come out just as you hope." He stared at me as I gave him a polite nod and turned my back on him.

I walked back to the grandstand as though I were treading air. I could almost feel the weight of six hundred dollars in crisp new bills pulling down my pocket. The thought crossed my mind that my ambiguous remarks to Wallens-Warhull might have been a trifle injudicious, but I rejected it. It was spring, the sun was shining, excitement and joy were in the air, and I would very soon be considerably better-to-do than I was now. Avaunt, dull care!

During the second, third, and fourth races, I divided my time between the grandstand and the paddock. Ten minutes before the fifth race, I entered the clubhouse again. Harrison Cobb was standing by himself near the windows that overlooked the track, sipping a drink and staring out moodily.

"Good afternoon, Mr. Cobb," I greeted him. "You don't look like an owner anticipating the upset victory of his 30-to-1 long shot."

He turned to me with a frown. "Hello, Moretti. Maybe that's because I'm not anticipating it."

"You've lost faith in Bonnycastle, have you?"

"Haven't you, given his miserable record at Elizabeth? Oh, I'm hoping he won't disgrace himself. But if he comes in fifth or sixth, he'll have done all I expect of him."

"I've got a hunch he may do a bit better than that," I said.

"Well, I hope you're right. But I'll tell you, Moretti, if he comes in last again, that's the end of it. I won't be embarrassed by a loser in my stable. If he runs today like he did at Elizabeth, out he goes."

"You'll sell him?"

"Like a shot, for anything I can get." He emptied his glass and set it down on a table angrily. "I'm building something at Stillwater Farm, goddamn it! *Veni, vidi, vici* is what it says on my coat-of-arms. That means no losers need apply!"

What an actor the man is, I thought. "I was at the stable a while ago, but I didn't see Bonnycastle," I said. "Your trainer Wallens wouldn't let me."

"Oh?" Cobb answered, apparently without interest.

"But I understood his point of view. If I were in his shoes, I wouldn't want any reporters sniffing around either." I paused a moment and then went on, "I mean, upsetting the horses and all."

Cobb picked his empty glass up from the table. "Yes. Well, Moretti, if you'll excuse me, I think I have just about enough time to get a refill before post time." He walked away toward the bar.

I stared down at the track and reviewed the reasons I was sure Bonnycastle would win. The bugle called the horses to the post for the fifth race, and they paraded out of the paddock and on to the track. Bonnycastle was sixth in line. He looked neither more active nor more passive than any of the other horses. Out of the corner of my eyes, I saw Harrison Cobb return to a position by the windows twenty or thirty feet away from me. He joined a group already in place, one of whom, I noticed, was Eddie Terhune.

The roar of the crowd signaled the beginning of the race. For the first fifty yards, the horses were so closely massed it was impossible to locate Bonnycastle. Then, as they emerged from the first turn, I saw the purple and green of Stillwater Farm. Bonnycastle was third from last. They rounded the second turn and entered the backstretch. Bonnycastle began to move up. He overtook one horse and then another. His jockey's whip was rising and falling in a quick, steady rhythm. Going into the third turn, he was in fourth place.

"Come on, Bonnycastle," I cried.

Coming out of the third turn and entering the last, Bonnycastle did not change his relative position. At the beginning of the homestretch he was still fourth. The crowd was busy cheering the favorites, who were battling it out for the lead. "You can do it, Bonnycastle," I called encouragingly. "Stretch those legs, now!"

Suddenly one of the horses behind him surged forward, and Bonnycastle was in fifth place. This must have discouraged him, because the spring went out of his stride, and the two other horses behind passed him within the last fifty yards of the race.

He finished dead last.

I heard the groans and laughter, the excited hubbub of the throng around me as though from a great distance. *It's not possible*, I thought. *God wouldn't do this.* Automatically I took out my notebook and jotted down a brief description of the race. *Six hundred dollars I didn't win.* I broke the point of my pencil and stared at it helplessly. *Three dollars and eighty-four cents I have left till payday.* I put the broken pencil and the notebook away carefully.

"You look like you've just lost your last friend, assuming you have a last friend," said Edderly of the *Tribune,* who seemed to be standing beside me. "Would this be the time for that fortifying taste you promised me?"

I shook my head slowly. "I'm sorry—not right now."

I left the clubhouse and walked around to the back of the building. I wanted to get away from other people for a few minutes, to drink three or four fingers from my flask, and to rethink the Bonnycastle problem and discover where I had gone wrong.

The area behind the clubhouse seemed to be used for the storage of bricks and lumber. There were stacks of each, covered with tarpaulins, as well as troughs for mixing cement and a number of wheelbarrows stacked in an orderly row. I sat down on a pile of one-by-twelves and unpocketed my flask. The sounds of the racetrack from beyond the building seemed far away. I was completely alone.

I swallowed the whiskey and felt it burn its way down to my belly and begin radiating warmth from there. *Bonnycastle will never race again under the Stillwater Farm colors—Cobb swore that to me, and he wouldn't have lied, because he expects me to print it in* The Spirit of the Times. *The odds were 30 to 1— they'll never be better than that. The horses were switched—I saw that with my own eyes. Matt Wallens is really Sailor Warhull, warned off every major American track for doping horses . . .*

Two men came around the side of the building. My first feeling was one of irritation, at what I took to be an accidental invasion of my privacy. Then I looked more closely, and the hair stood up on the back of my neck.

The man in front was Sharkey, whom I had last seen at the Circus. He was smiling sleepily. His left hand slipped over his right as if he were pulling on a glove. The man beside him was unfamiliar—a fat face, a crooked jaw, a suit too tight for him. As they came toward me they moved apart, so that I would be placed between them.

"Mr. Klepp is disappointed in you. You didn't remember what he said," Sharkey said conversationally. The brass knuckles gleamed in the sunlight. His companion hunched his shoulders and opened and closed his hands. I noticed that his white shirt was almost black around the collar.

"Wait a minute: What are you talking about?" I cried as I took a half-step backward and felt the stacked lumber press against my calves.

"Mr. Klepp warned you. He told you not to snoop in his affairs no more. He told you what would happen if you did." Sharkey might have been talking about the prospect of a walk through Central Park on a pleasant afternoon. He and his associate moved toward me from both sides.

I started to scramble backward up the lumber. "Snooping? Who's been snooping? I'm out here earning my daily bread. I wouldn't snoop on Mr. Klepp for the world!"

"Mr. Klepp heard you went to see Mrs. Kanady today. He kind of thought that was snooping. Too bad."

I was now sitting atop the pile of lumber and trying to pull my legs under me. Before I could, however, the fat man grabbed my ankles. "You ain't going nowhere," he said, leaning back with my feet tightly held under his arms.

Sharkey raised his right arm as my legs straightened. The brass knuckles gleamed murderously on his fist. *Mother of God! I* thought, *he's going to smash my kneecaps!* I twisted my body with all my strength as his fist descended. I felt the paralyzing impact of the blow on my thigh.

The fat man continued to pull backwards on my legs, and before Sharkey could launch another blow, I slid off the pile of lumber. My back struck the ground, and one of my feet was suddenly free. The fat man leaned forward to secure it again, and I kicked him in the face. His mouth split open.

Sharkey threw himself upon me, pinning my chest and shoulders. "Hold his legs, goddamn it!" he grunted. The fat man grabbed at my free foot, and I kicked at his head again. My heel caught him on the ear. He gave a whimpering sound of pain and rage and fell forward on top of me, immobilizing me from the waist down.

Sharkey's face was six inches from mine. His sleepy eyes were wide open, the whites laced with red, the pupils no larger than pinheads. "Now you get it, Moretti. For keeps," he snarled. He held my head against the ground with his left forearm as he drew his right hand back. I strained against the pressure but couldn't move an inch. I closed my eyes instinctively as I waited for the blow.

A moment passed before I opened them again to the sound of

an odd gurgling noise. Sharkey's face was drawn back from mine, his jaw tilted up, his skin darkening, and his mouth agape. A white silk scarf was twisted around his neck. My eyes moved up the scarf to the hands that held it, and then to the face above them. It was Tomaso. He was wearing a light overcoat, buttoned to the neck. Beside him was Gaetano, with a long, slender knife in his hand, knees bent as he crouched over the fat man.

Tomaso twisted the silken garrote tighter, and Sharkey made a rattling sound in his throat. Gaetano pressed the point of his knife under the fat man's chin. "Are you all right, Patrizio?" Tomaso asked grimly.

I struggled to a sitting position. "God, don't kill them!" I gasped. "What if the police should come? They'd put us in jail for life!"

"Are you hurt?" Tomaso insisted. "If you are hurt, they must be hurt. Don Paolo would want it." Sharkey's eyeballs were bulging and his face was the color of fresh calves' liver; the fat man made sounds like a dog whining outside a closed door.

I shook my head and got to my feet. The ground was unsteady, and I leaned on the pile of lumber for support. "No, I'm fine," I said. "They didn't lay a glove on me. Just take their brass knuckles away from them and make them go away."

Tomaso drew Sharkey to his feet with the scarf. "Don't move or I'll twist your head off," he ordered. He tugged the brass knuckles off Sharkey's fist and pocketed them. He ran his hand over Sharkey's pockets and produced a spring-loaded knife with a five-inch blade, which he broke under his heel. Meanwhile Gaetano relieved the fat man of a slung shot and a small nickel-plated revolver.

"What d'ya say, Patrizio? Want to give them something to remember you by?" Tomaso asked, giving the twisted silk scarf a half-turn.

I shook my head. "No, just get rid of them."

Tomaso shrugged. "You're the doctor." He drew back his free arm and struck Sharkey a powerful blow over the left kidney.

"Remember me, *porco*. Next time I see you, it's the *lupara*. You won't have no face left when they bury you." Gaetano eased the pressure of his knife point, and the fat man scrambled to his feet. I was glad to see his split mouth was bleeding on his dirty collar. "Go," Tomaso said, untwisting the scarf with a flip of his wrist.

Without a backward glance, Sharkey walked toward the corner of the building with the fat man behind him. Just before he turned the corner, Sharkey glanced over his shoulder at me. His heavy-lidded eyes were expressionless. I knew that if there had been a small chance he would ever have forgotten me before, there was no chance at all now.

When they were gone, Tomaso belched comfortably as he tied the scarf around his neck. "They won't try nothing else today, *paesano*. Tomorrow, who knows?" He pressed his fingers against the silk in a futile effort to eradicate the wrinkles. "But I think, now they know about us, they will try to kill you next time. Killing a man is easier than breaking his kneecaps."

I swallowed.

"Of course they know we will kill them if they do, so perhaps they will kill us first. If they followed you to Don Paolo's, they know where to find us. We know where to find them. This Klepp, when he learns what happened today, will know that killing you will start a war. Is killing you worth starting a war for?"

"Not to me it's not!" I cried fervently.

He looked at me appraisingly. "I agree—but I am not this whoremaster Klepp. Ah, well, we'll see, won't we, Gaetano?" He clapped his colleague on the shoulder. "Are you going back to Manhattan now, Patrizio?"

"No, I've got a few more races to report this afternoon."

"We'll be here as long as you are. *Addio, amico*." The tall Sicilian and the slight Gypsy sauntered around the side of the building and disappeared, and I found myself alone again. I heard the sound of a cheer from the crowd, as remote as music across a lake. My thigh ached. I thought about Sharkey's brass knuckles. *One rap on each knee,* I thought, *and it would have been a wheelchair from here on out.*

The loneliness of this forgotten spot behind the clubhouse was suddenly unnerving. I wanted to be in the middle of a shouting, laughing crowd intent on nothing more lethal than a horse race. Limping slightly, I made my way back to the grandstand.

During the remainder of the racing day, I stayed in my seat and made faithful notes on each race as it was run. I did not search the stand around me for either Sharkey and the fat man or Tomaso and Gaetano. If any or all of them were within sight, I did not want to know it.

The last race ended a little after five o'clock, and I joined the thousands of other passengers crowding the cars back to Manhattan. I was lucky enough to get a window seat, but took little advantage of it; most of the trip I spent with my eyes closed and my head in my hands. My mind was a kaleidoscope, and no matter how I turned it, the pieces fell into baffling disarray. I retraced my steps from the first time I entered Zum Groben Michel and made the acquaintance of Maisie, Marya, and Sasha. I relived my visit to Stillwater Farm Stables, my meeting with Cobb and his wife, and the Kanadys and Eddie Terhune, and Matt Wallens in the stable. I remembered Bonnycastle nuzzling my hand with his velvet muzzle—a Bonnycastle with a wen in the corner of his eye. I remembered the meeting in Union Square —Tim Kanady's rage, the charging mounted police, Marya Perlman's ominous prophecy, and my shock at its fulfillment two days later. I remembered Marya in my rooms—I remembered a good deal about Marya in my rooms. I remembered Hochmuth feeding his pigeons, and Axel Klepp running his business, and Uncle Paolo caring about his family.

I sensed a connection, an underlying pattern, but turn the kaleidoscope as often as I might, I couldn't find it among the unrelated bits of colored glass. What had anarchists to do with a racing stable? Who could relate the elegant Florence Kanady to the sinister brothel called the Circus? Why would a horse that had been carefully prepared to win a crucial race at long odds lose the race instead? I groaned and shook my head.

I was still shaking it forty-five minutes later as I walked along Chambers Street toward the office of *The Spirit of the Times.* I was still a dozen paces from the entrance when I heard a husky voice murmur, "Moretti, stop a minute."

It was Blinky Malone, the blind pencil-and-shoelace vendor who plied his trade in front of the office every day from eight to five. "Hello, Blinky," I said. "It's way after closing time. What are you doing out here?"

He clutched his tray close to his chest and leaned toward me. "Don't go inside," he whispered. "They're waiting for you."

"What do you mean? Who's waiting for me?"

He leaned even closer, and I felt his breath on my ear "The coppers. They come an hour ago. Two of them stayed inside, and the others left. They're gonna take you in."

I have never understood how Blinky, who is, I am sure, legitimately and totally blind, knows everything that happens on Chambers Street, but he does. I took his hand and squeezed it gratefully. "You're a prince, Blinky. Did they say anything about me—about what they want me for?"

He leaned closer yet, and his leathery lips touched my ear lobe. "Accessory after the fact—to murder," he breathed. "You'd best be getting out of here, Paddy. Quick."

I squeezed his hand again in farewell and began walking rapidly toward Broadway, keeping close to the inner edge of the sidewalk. *Accessory to murder!* I thought to myself, stunned. *They think I helped Marya blow up Tim Kanady! No, that wouldn't be accessory after the fact—they think I've helped Marya since the murder!*

And they're right! But how do they know?

At Broadway I caught an electric car headed north. It was almost empty, and I felt as conspicuous in its brightly lighted interior as a naked mannequin in a shop window. I pretended to be asleep with my head propped up on an open hand that covered most of my face.

I rode a block past Bleeker Street before I got off and then walked west to McDougal Street and south back to Bleeker. The street seemed deserted. I waited in the shadow a minute before continuing toward my building.

The chandelier in the foyer threw a warm rectangle of yellow on the sidewalk. I had almost reached it when I sensed a movement in a dark areaway on my left. Before I could react, a hand gripped my arm fiercely, and I found myself flying through the air into the areaway. My shoulders slammed into a brick wall, and as I opened my mouth to cry out, I felt something very thinly edged press against my throat.

"So you sold her for thirty pieces of silver—you bastard!" growled a voice from the darkness. "For that, *spion*, you die!" I felt the blade begin to move.

"Wait, for the love of God!" I cried in a stifled voice. "Is that you, Sasha? Sasha, listen! I *helped* her! I gave her a place to stay! I'm her friend!" The knife-edge continued to press into my flesh but stopped moving. I went on, "Sasha, I don't know what's happened. When I left this morning, Marya was safe in my rooms. As far as I know she could still be there—I haven't been back yet. But the police are looking for me. I'm a fugitive as much as she is."

The cold, thin pressure on my throat eased. "How did they know she was here?" Sasha asked harshly. "Nobody knew that but you."

"You knew, didn't you?" I parried. He didn't answer, so I went on, "I don't know how they knew. Maybe the landlady told them—maybe somebody saw her through a window." I put my hand on his wrist and gently depressed the knife until it was safely away from my neck. "When did the police come for her?"

In the darkly shadowed areaway, I could make out only the silhouette of his body—the ears projecting from the round head, the broad shoulders that dwarfed the slight torso and legs. The rage seemed to go out of him; the head bowed and the shoulders slumped. I heard a click as he closed the knife and slipped it into his pocket. "This afternoon, about four," he answered dully. "They took her away in a Black Maria."

"Were you here to see it?"

"No, I heard about it from a comrade who saw them taking her into Centre Street. I've been here ever since, though, waiting for you to come home."

I told how I had been warned that the police were waiting for me at the newspaper office. "Furthermore, two brawny lads tried to pop my kneecaps at Gravesend this afternoon, and now you come within a quarter of an inch of slitting my throat. I feel I've been the object of considerable attentions."

"The cossacks will hang here," Sasha groaned. "They will convict her of killing that Tammany swine Kanady, and they will hang her, and the bourgeois world will applaud her death. *Ach, Gott!*"

I touched his shoulder. "Maybe not. They haven't got *us* yet. The Moretti is still at large. It's not as if I'm totally without experience in this kind of brouhaha. The most desperate gunfighters in Kansas will tell you that I'm not the man to be underestimated when the chips are down."

He made a gesture of despair. "What can you do against the entire capitalist system?"

"I can't tell you that now," I replied truthfully. "Now listen, Sasha. If I need to get a message to you, how can I do it?" I was answered by a suspicious silence. "Man, I may need your help!" I said urgently. "You and I are the only chance Marya has, remember."

Unwillingly he muttered, "Broome Street, between Mott and Elizabeth. The butcher shop. Ask for Karl. He can reach me."

"You wouldn't have any money to spare, would you?" I asked. I saw his head shake in the darkness. "Well, it can't be helped. Stay here a minute or two till I'm gone." I stepped back onto the sidewalk. Keeping close to the masonry, I walked away quickly. At the corner I turned left, heading into the maze of narrow streets that makes up Greenwich Village.

Tomorrow's Sunday, I thought as I walked along the empty sidewalks. *There's nothing to be done till Monday. I can't go to the office, or home. I have $3.84 to my name. If I keep walking the streets, it's only a matter of time until the police pick me up. It's 8:00 P.M. Saturday. Where can I go?*

I could only think of one place.

8

*A Commanding Figure
in the
World of Journalism*

AT THE CORNER of Dover and Pearl streets, in the shadow of
Brooklyn Bridge, stands the seven-story monument to enterprise
and vanity known as the Richard K. Fox Building. It has been
called the Sporting Center of the World. It is the home of the
National Police Gazette, loved in every barber shop and cursed
from every pulpit in America, and as much a sanctuary to hard-
pressed journalists as Notre Dame was to the fugitives of medie-
val Paris.

As I approached the building, I could make out the painted
signs between the floors by the light of the street lamp on the
corner—NATIONAL POLICE GAZETTE—RICHARD K. FOX, PUB-
LISHER—JOB PRINTING —ART-ENGRAVING—DEEDS & DOCU-
MENTS. The first two floors were lighted, the others dark. I
entered the front door and climbed the wide stairs to the second-
floor reception area, where I stopped a moment to marvel at the
appointments, as I did every time I visited Fox's Xanadu. It was
a very large room, paneled in mahogany, cherry, and teak,
lighted by four great chandeliers that were masterpieces of
sparkling glass and metal. With its deep-pile carpeting and luxuri-

ous red leather armchairs, it looked like a room furnished for the clientele of a bank rather than a newspaper.

The walls that surrounded the reception area were lined with glass display cases in which many of the trophies Fox regularly awarded to athletes and pseudoathletes were displayed; the publisher gave public recognition not only to prize fighters, rowers, fencers, and runners but to one-legged dancers, rat catchers, and champion oyster openers as well. Anything that could be made the basis for an unusual story was grist to Fox's mill.

The room was empty. I walked through it to a corridor at the rear, the soft swoosh of my footsteps in the carpeting sounding loud in my ears. Halfway down the corridor on the right was a door, behind which I could hear the muffled sound of voices. I turned the knob, entered, and let the door close behind me. It gave a sharp click as the lock snapped home.

"My God, Moretti! What disaster brings you to the Black Hole of Calcutta?" asked Pomerance of the *World*, a bespectacled little man with a pot belly and feet that formed a one-hundred-forty-degree angle with each other. He was fixing himself a towering sandwich at the buffet table.

"Living beyond your means again?" inquired Howell of the *Sun*, as he poured an inch of whiskey from a cut-glass decanter into a glass. He pulled down on his lower lip to expose tobacco-stained teeth. "Some people never learn they have to pay the piper. Eh, Gans?"

Gans of the *Evening Post* was sitting at a desk by the wall and sucking at the end of a penholder. He took it out of his mouth breifly to answer, "Libertines— couldn't make ends meet if they were paid twelve dollars a week."

I glanced around the room. In addition to Pomerance, Howell, and Gans, two other men were there: a young man with blood-shot eyes and a gray complexion, whom I had never seen before, and an older man, whose name was Sawyer or Sadler or Sanders, asleep and snoring on one of the couches. The buffet was well stocked with beef, turkey, potato salad, cheese, and bread. A smaller table held decanters and bottles of whiskey and wine, glasses, and an insulated bucket of ice. Around the walls were six desks, each supplied with paper, pen, and ink, one occupied by Gans, the other five empty. I tried the door through which I had entered, although I knew it would be locked.

I crossed to the small table and mixed myself a generous whiskey and water. I took a swallow and then made a gesture with my hand encompassing the room. "I don't really need this, you understand," I said loftily. "I have three dollars and eighty-four cents."

"Braggart," said Howell. "After investing twenty-five dollars in the four, five, seven, and eight of clubs in the laughable belief that the six would materialize, I have exactly thirty-seven cents."

"If I had three dollars and eighty-four cents, I'd be eating at Delmonico's," said Pomerance over the top of his sandwich.

Of all the charitable institutions in New York City, the one most appreciated by the working press was this room in the *Police Gazette* building. Whenever any newspaperman found himself without funds over the weekend, he could, if he chose, repair to Fox's hospice, where there was good plain food to eat, enough liquor to keep his fires of inspiration burning but not quenched, a desk to work at, and a couch to rest on when his labors were completed. The door by which he entered was locked on the outside until Richard Fox himself opened it on Monday morning, when he presented each of the room's occupants with a ten-dollar bill in exchange for the story he had written.

I carried my glass to an empty desk and picked up the sheet of paper lying there. It was the headline for the "Horrors" column, a regular feature of the *Police Gazette*.

HOMICIDAL HORRORS

Of Sufficient Number and Variety
of Atrocity to Enable the Craving
of the Most Exacting

TO FILL TO SATIETY

A Sickening and Sanguinary Recital
of the Murderous Tendency of Mankind,
Which Should Afford

A FIELD FOR THE HUMANITARIAN

Beside it was the penciled notation, "Need additional items for this. R. D. F." I picked up a pen and tapped it on the desk top thoughtfully.

"Have any of you lads written up the Tim Kanady bombing for 'Horrors'?" I asked. I was answered by a chorus of negatives. *Well, why not?* I thought. *Maybe I can cast some doubt on the official version.* I set to work, first describing the bombing at Tammany Hall as gorily as possible, then the May Day riot that had preceded it, with much emphasis on the march of the *filles de joie.* I included Marya Perlman's malediction, but immediately followed it with "The theory of the guilt of the Perlman woman, however, while representing the unimaginative police viewpoint, is widely disputed by knowledgeable political and journalistic sources. The finger of guilt, they assert confidently, will finally and truly be leveled at certain whited sepulchres whose public facade of righteousness conceals the charnel stench of sin."

I finished the piece and read it over. Pleased with the result, I strolled to the buffet and fixed myself a generous plate of rare roast beef and potato salad. I poured myself a glass of burgundy and carried my repast to a comfortable armchair, where I ate and drank slowly while I chatted with Howell and Pomerance.

Too soon the food was gone and I was too full to eat any more. Pomerance moved his seat to one of the desks and began writing, and Howell excused himself to visit the adjoining bathroom. I looked at my watch and found it was only a few minutes after ten. If I went to sleep now, I reflected, I would wake up by seven in the morning, slept out, with the whole Sunday stretching out in front of me. There was no help for it—I might as well write Richard Fox another story or two. Grumbling to myself at the unscrupulous system the publisher of the *Police Gazette* had devised to provide himself with low-cost copy, I returned to my desk.

I wrote for two hours, spinning a largely imaginary tale of the white slavery trade which featured Red Light Lizzie and Jane the Grabber, two actual procuresses who had warred for control of New York prostitution a decade before. When I finished it, I mixed myself a nightcap and stretched out on a couch with the glass balanced on my chest. All the other reporters were asleep except Sawyer or Sadler or Sanders, who was writing diligently and muttering to himself. I sipped my whiskey and felt drowsiness creep over my body. It was only this morning that I had left Marya Perlman in my flat and paid a visit to Mulberry Bend—it seemed incredible that so much could have happened in the interim. Uncle Paolo, Flo Kanady, Harrison Cobb, and Matt Wallens, the disastrous bet on Bonnycastle—I interrupted the chain of memory to strengthen myself with a swallow of whiskey —Sharkey and his fat friend behind the clubhouse, the happy intervention of Tomaso and Gaetano, Blinky Malone's warning and Sasha's knife at my throat. And now temporary sanctuary, but after this, what? When I had to leave the *Police Gazette* building, could I even stay out of the hands of the police or Axel Klepp's minions, let alone discover anything to help Marya escape from a murder charge?

My thigh ached. I drank some more of my whiskey and was surprised to discover I had emptied the glass. I considered the effort involved in getting up to fix myself another drink and decided it was too high a price to pay. I set the glass on the floor beside me, closed my eyes, and took a deep breath.

When I awoke it was almost nine o'clock in the morning, and my fellow inmates were all awake, eating, drinking, joking, laughing, and behaving in a generally noisy manner. I groaned and turned my face to the back of the couch. Gans observed my movement. "Hey, up and at 'em, Moretti," he called jovially. "Get yourself some dog hair and sing us a song."

"How about 'God Damn the Lane Hotel'?" asked Pomerance. "I've always thought it was one of your most sensitive renditions."

Sawyer or Sadler or Sanders held up two sugar cubes, the sides of which he had marked with ink spots in number from one to six. "That $3.84 of yours, Moretti—I know how you could increase it by another dollar and a half!"

Since further sleep was obviously impossible, I sat up and put my feet on the floor. "Just don't all scream," I said. "It's like waking up in a cage full of hyenas." I tasted the inside of my mouth with my tongue and found it unappetizing. I got up from the couch and limped to the buffet, which was sadly depleted. I made a turkey and cheese sandwich and took a bite; the bread was stale.

"Maybe you'd rather favor us with 'McCann He Was a Rounder,' " Pomerance suggested.

I took another bite and decided that if I were to get the sandwich down at all I would have to add moisture to the operation. I poured myself a glass of wine. After that the food went down much easier.

About noon, after I had lost $3.84 to Sawyer or Sadler or Sanders and exhausted my musical repertoire, the door to the hallway opened to admit a newcomer and closed behind him with its inflexible click. It was Edderly, the racing columnist from the *Tribune*. His eyes were more bloodshot than they had been the day before, and the expression on his long-chinned face was hangdog.

"She threw me out, boys," he announced without preamble.

"I came in stinking of whiskey at nine o'clock in the morning, crawled in like a hound that's rolled in his own vomit, and she threw me out of the house, God love her. And why shouldn't she? 'Let's see your paycheck,' she says, and I haven't got any paycheck. I've spent it all carousing in filthy holes, buying drinks for whores and spongers."

"Hello, Edderly," I said. "You better have a sandwich and a drink."

"The kid's been coughing so much lately, I thought I'd just get out of the house for a few minutes, just go down to the corner for one glass of beer. I planned to be back in fifteen minutes, honest to God I did. Nine o'clock in the morning! God, what a bastard I am."

I took him by the elbow and led him to the buffet. "Fix yourself something to eat, man, and have a drop to wash it down. Then write Fox a story and make yourself ten dollars and take it home to her as a down payment on your new devotional attitude."

"A hound that's rolled in his own vomit," he repeated lugubriously, laying slices of turkey on a piece of pumpernickel. "No wonder I'm offensive to her. How could I respect her if she wasn't offended by me?" He poured himself a glass of whiskey and tossed it down. "You think she'd take my ten dollars, Moretti?"

"I'm certain of it." I led him to a chair and sat him down. "Now relax, eat your sandwich, and think wholesome thoughts." To distract him, I went on, "What's it like in the outside world? I feel like I've been locked up here longer than the Count of Monte Cristo."

He swallowed a bite of his sandwich and regarded it dubiously. "The same as always. Birds singing. The sun shining. People with clear consciences going to church. Rotten lechers and drunks peering out of darkened doorways. Newsboys shouting the headlines from their extras . . ."

"Extras? There's an extra on the street?"

"All about the new anarchist outrage. Another of the Tammany sachems got himself blown up."

A sudden tingle ran through my body. I yawned to mask my excitement. "Oh? They do keep doing that, don't they? What happened this time?"

"Fellow blown up in his own home, last evening sometime. The bomb was delivered in a hollowed-out book. Open the cover and ka-powie." He started to rise from his chair. "I need another drink to get this sandwich down, Moretti."

I pushed him back into his chair. "Allow me." I refilled his glass and returned. "I don't suppose you remember who the Tammany sachem was?" I asked.

"Name of Terhune, Eddie Terhune. I met him once. A lawyer. I suppose they'll blow up Boss Crocker next."

"Well, it's good they're concentrating on a dispensable section of society," I said lightly. "Who did they say did it?"

"I don't know," he said without interest. "Moretti, do you think she'll really take me back? By God, if she will, I'll guarantee never to touch another drop of whiskey as long as I live!"

Try as I might, I couldn't get any additional facts out of him. After a few minutes of trying, I persuaded him to move to a desk and begin composing a story about the Trunk Murderer of Staten Island. Then I lay down on a couch to discourage conversation and reflected on the meaning of this second assassination.

Marya was in police custody before Terhune was killed— Sasha said they picked her up about four in the afternoon, I thought. *Then they must know she didn't do it? Wrong. She could have arranged for the bomb to be sent at any earlier time. But what would her motive have been? She had a reason to kill Kanady—the May Day troubles in Union Square. But why would she want to kill Terhune? Answer: weren't both men in Tammany Hall, both important figures in the political organization that controls New York City, the organization that every radical and reformer believes to be the country's most corrupt machine? Isn't that reason enough for an anarchist to want to see them dead?*

"Hey, Moretti," Howell called. "You in for a game of stud? I'll give you ten dollar's credit."

I mumbled a sleepy negative and shifted position on the couch. A new thought occurred to me. If the police had been looking for me as an accomplice after the fact for Kanady's murder, what would their attitude toward me be now? There was not much doubt of the answer: they would want me more now than before.

And what would they do to Marya, now that they had their hands on her? Could they wring a confession out of her? No — if there was one thing I was sure of in a world full of uncertainty, it was that nobody would ever get Marya Perlman to confess to a crime of which she was not guilty. Or to deny responsibility for a crime of which she *was* guilty, for that matter.

Then who had killed Kanady? Who had killed Terhune? The killings appeared to be connected; were they? If so, what was the motive?

The poker game started with noisy banter that continued to grow in volume. After a few minutes, I heard Edderly protest from his desk, and the gamblers restrained themselves briefly. When their voices rose again, I gave a loud groan and put a pillow over my head.

It's no good, I thought. *You can't stay flat on your back till tomorrow morning. If you did go to sleep now, you'd be awake all night.* I sat up with a curse and stamped my feet on the floor. "All right, you pismires, deal me in," I said.

The ten dollars worth of credit Howell allowed me held up very well for the first two hours; at one point, I was thirty-three dollars ahead. Then the young man with the bloodshot eyes and gray complexion, whom the others called Settlemeyer, chose a wild-card game. The player who dealt after him also called for wild cards, and the inexorable slide from skill to chance began.

In spite of my protests, we were soon playing games in which one-eyed jacks and split-whiskered kings and deuces and treys and ultimately a quarter of the deck was wild, in which fours brought extra cards and threes required the doubling of the pot, in which the high hand and the low hand would split the winnings and a full house rarely qualified as either. I watched my thirty-three dollars being eroded by this idiocy, powerless to put a stop to it.

The moment arrived when I had to decide whether my four aces, which were actually one ace, one trey, one deuce, and one split-whiskered king, were worth a call against Pomerance, who had a natural pair and a wild card showing. I pushed in my last two dollars and said, "I call." He had five of a kind. I cursed him bitterly and went to the buffet table, where I found a slice of cheese and a heel of bread. I made an open-faced sandwich, which I washed down with a glass of whiskey. Then, for lack of anything else to do, I sat down at a desk and wrote Fox another story.

Somehow the day wore on, and evening arrived, and I was tired enough to go to sleep again.

The door finally opened at 8:30 the next morning, and no prisoner in the Tombs was ever happier at his release than I. Richard K. Fox, his formidable waxed mustache curled up to place his nose in parentheses, stood in the doorway. He wore a flawlessly tailored blue pinstripe suit of English cut, a foulard cravat with a large diamond stickpin, and gray spats over gleaming patent leather oxfords. "Payday, gentlemen!" he called in his melodious tenor voice that still carried a touch of the brogue.

We inmates quickly formed a line, each of us with the stories written during the period of incarceration. Fox glanced over each story quickly, signaled his approval with a word or two, and handed the writer a crisp new ten-dollar bill. I was fourth in line. Fox looked at me sharply a moment as he took the sheets from my hand. "Moretti? Quite a surprise to see you here," he said. He glanced down at the stories I had given him. The account of Tim Kanady's murder was on top. His eyes moved down the page rapidly, and then he looked at me again. "Just step to one side, Mr. Moretti," he said as he handed me my ten dollars. "I'd like a word with you, if you don't mind."

Before I could tuck the banknote into my pocket, it disappeared into the clutches of Howell, who grinned wolfishly and said, "Congratulations—your credit's good again!" One by one, he and the others made their way down the corridor to the reception area until I was left alone with the publisher.

"If you've a moment to spare, Mr. Moretti, perhaps you might join me in my office," he said, tucking his hand under my elbow and guiding me gently toward the staircase. We ascended to the third floor, where he escorted me into a huge room whose furnishings were dominated by an oil portrait ten feet high of Richard K. Fox in a Napoleonic pose. He motioned me to a comfortable leather armchair and took his seat behind a vast desk, absolutely bare except for the manuscript sheets he tossed upon it.

He touched the tips of his fingers and regarded me over them. "This story about Tim Kanady's taking-off—you have a very interesting slant here." I thanked him. He went on, "You say the police theory, which you characterize as—" He consulted my story. "—unimaginative, you say this theory is widely disputed by knowledgeable political and journalistic sources. Would it be too much to ask which political and journalistic sources you have reference to?"

I hesitated a moment before answering, "*This* political and journalistic source."

His eyes glinted like agates, and his gaze was unwinking. "I see. And these certain whited sepulchres you mention, whose public facade of righteousness conceals the charnel stench of sin —that has a fine ring to it, Moretti!—what whited sepulchres might those be?"

"To tell you the plain, exact truth, Mr. Fox, I'm not prepared to say at this time."

The corner of his thin lips twisted slightly. "But you will be prepared to say at some time in the future?"

"I certainly hope so," I said fervently.

"I hope so too, if I run this story." He continued to regard me thoughtfully. "Moretti, let me tell you something you may or may not know. The anarchist Perlman woman, whose responsibility for Kanady's assassination you question, was apprehended by the police Saturday afternoon at a flat on Bleeker Street rented by a reporter for *The Spirit of the Times*." He paused to allow me to speak, and when I didn't, he resumed. "Four or five hours later another denizen of Tammany Hall, Eddie Terhune by name, was dispatched to his ancestors by means of another bomb, which was delivered to his home in a hollowed-out book. Would you care to guess what the book was, Moretti?"

I said I didn't think I would.

"It was *The Spirit of the Times*'s annual racing yearbook. I'd say that was a noteworthy coincidence, wouldn't you?" He touched one finger to his mustache and followed its waxen curve to a point an inch from his right eye. With a thin smile, he continued, "Can you think of any reason why I shouldn't summon the police to this office and turn you over to them this very instant?"

I raised my chin and tried for an appearance of Integrity with its back to the wall. "Because as God is my judge I am innocent of any crime, Mr. Fox."

"I see." He moved his finger to the other side of his face and traced the curve of his mustache to a point an inch from his left eye. "I think it would be advisable to tell me everything you know about this case. At that point I may be better able to decide a citizen's duty under the circumstances."

I drew a deep breath and began my story, beginning with my meeting with Marya and Sasha at Zum Groben Michel. I left out nothing except certain personal details concerning Marya's and my activities at my apartment, and from the glint in Fox's eyes as I hurried past them, I needn't have bothered.

When I had finished, he rose from his chair and began to pace the floor, his slender body angled forward and his hands clasped behind him. "And what are your plans when you leave this office, Moretti? Assuming you have any plans, which apparently you haven't had heretofore."

I explained my belief that Kanady had been murdered for reasons other than his calling out the police in Union Square. "What other reasons?" Fox demanded. I said I hadn't yet been able to investigate all of Kanady's connections, but that there were at least three areas that seemed to offer promise—his alleged financial interest in the Circus, his wife's relationship to Eddie Terhune, and his acquaintance with Harrison Cobb, proprietor of Stillwater Farm Stables.

Fox questioned me closely on each area and shook his head at my unsatisfactory answers. "So what it boils down to is that his wife said he was in business with this Axel Klepp, that you saw Eddie Terhune give somebody a hug coming out of the Kanady house, and that Kanady was Cobb's guest at his farm and at the Elizabeth racetrack. Correct?"

"I think I have a little more than that," I said stiffly.

"You think! You think!" Fox cried. "Now you listen to me, Moretti! I probably know more about crime and criminals in New York City than any man alive, including Chief Inspector Byrnes himself. From the moment I took this paper over as a bad debt and decided to make it the premier police publication in the world, I have eaten, drunk, slept, and breathed crime and corruption!" He turned to the huge portrait behind his desk and gestured toward it dramatically. "That man you see there, raised in Belfast with an empty belly and barely enough shirt to tuck into his pants, became the Richard K. Fox known to presidents and kings the world over for one reason and one reason only! *Because he knows crime!*" He glared at me fiercely. "Would you agree to that, Moretti?"

"Yes, sir, I certainly would."

"Then let me tell you something about crime—especially crime in New York City. *It doesn't exist unless you can prove it*! At least, it doesn't exist outside of the lower classes. Dagoes and micks and greasers and niggers and chinks commit crimes, we all know that. Anarchists commit crimes. Pimps and prostitutes commit crimes. Gangs like the Whyos have a standard price list —two dollars for a plain beating, fifteen dollars for chewing off an ear, a hundred dollars for the big job. The Mafia and the Camorra tie people up and put them in barrels so they'll strangle themselves. Gypsies can rob you by osmosis. But upper-class people? Prove it, Moretti!"

He took a turn around the room, then resumed. "I don't mean just prove it. I mean prove it, and then prove it some more, and then *prove* that you've proved it. Because that's what it takes to convict a criminal who doesn't belong to what we like to think of as the criminal classes! We make it hard, because it upsets us to think that people who wash behind their ears and know which fork to use at dinner may also deserve to dance at the end of a rope!"

I kept quiet because I wasn't sure what he wanted me to say, if anything. He walked to a window that looked north toward the Lower East Side and the fashionable neighborhoods beyond it. "People talk about sinful cities, Moretti," he said ruminatively. "Marseilles—Port Said—Macao and Hong Kong—Limehouse in London and the Casbah in Algiers—Let me tell you, not one of them can hold a candle to little old New York. Everything corrupt ever conceived by the mind of man is for sale within a radius of five miles from this office. It's all on the market, and most of it is bought and paid for by members of the Uppah Clawses. The people who secretly finance whorehouses, and have affairs with socially prominent matrons, and are the guests of Long Island horsemen."

I thought it was time to say something. "Yes, sir," I said.

"Now, at the present time, Moretti, the police are satisfied they know who killed Tim Kanady. It was the Perlman woman, a notorious anarchist criminal who made a public threat against him only two days before he died. They have her in custody, and they would have had her earlier if it wasn't for a wiseacre newspaper reporter who made himself an accessory after the fact by hiding her in his apartment.

"But they don't just want the newspaper reporter as an accessory. Since Saturday night, they also want to question him on another killing, of which his good friend the anarchist woman is certainly innocent, since she was in police custody at the time."

"The fact that she is innocent hardly makes me guilty, Mr. Fox!"

He looked at me pityingly. "There's a point I perhaps did not make sufficiently clear. When I was listing those members of the lower classes who are considered the source of metropolitan criminality—pimps and prostitutes and thugs and Gypsies and the rest—I omitted to mention one group many respectable people consider the most heinous of the lot: newspaper reporters. It is not a question of deciding *if* newspaper reporters are guilty — of course they are! It is only a question of *which* guilt they will be charged with!"

I slumped in my chair with my chin touching my chest. "You're telling me I'm in a hopeless position, then?" I asked. "You think I should turn myself in?"

Fox unbuttoned three buttons on his waistcoat and thrust his hand through the opening. He drew himself to his full five feet four inches of height. His eyes flashed. "I did not become the commanding figure I am in the world of journalism by counseling surrender, Moretti. By no means! When you came to the *Police Gazette* building for sanctuary, you chose more wisely than you knew! Although I am far from satisfied that you know what you're doing—actually quite the reverse, as a matter of fact— I propose to do what I can to enable you to stay out of the clutches of the police as long as possible!"

I raised my chin from my chest. "Mr. Fox! I don't know how to thank you!"

"I do. I consider this a quid pro quo. In the unlikely event that you discover the murderer or murderers of Kanady and Terhune, and he or they are other than Marya Perlman or yourself, I will expect a complete account of the whole affair, written in your best 'whited sepulchre' style, in time for my earliest subsequent issue." He paused to consider his terms, then added, "In case you are captured in spite of my best efforts, I expect a brief death-house statement."

"I'll give you the story, but I can't write it under my own by-line, sir. That's my agreement with *The Spirit of the Times.*"

Fox removed his hand from his vest and touched his mustache with his fingertip. "Forgive me, Moretti," he said kindly, "but your by-line is not Richard Harding Davis. You may sign yourself any way or no way, as long as your account is more or less factual. It is a matter of no concern to me."

"Yes, sir." My chin touched my chest again.

Fox clapped his hands. "Very well, let's get at it. The problem is fixing you up so you can move freely through the city without being recognized by the police, correct? Very good. I think this calls for Kouradin." He crossed the room to the door, opened it, and shouted, "Get me Kouradin up here!" He closed the door and said to me, "Kouradin is our theater man." Before he could get back to his desk, the door opened again, and a slender man with thin hair, expressive hands, and very thick-lensed spectacles entered.

"You wanted to see me, Mr. Fox?" he asked in a nervous tremolo.

Fox pointed to me and explained the problem. The disguise should be such that it would pass inspection by the police, some of whom might be expected to know me by sight, and would allow me to move freely anywhere in the city without seeming out-of-place.

Kouradin walked in a circle around me, peering myopically at my face and tapping his fingertips together. "Of course. Yes, indeed. Certainly," he cried. "A nun? No, not unless there were two of him. Also his face would be too open—nuns don't have beards. And I do think we want a beard—beards are so concealing. Now, who wears beards?"

"Presidents?" I offered.

He sniffed at me. "Old soldiers? Capitalists? Poets and artists? Bowery derelicts?"

"Remember, he has to move around the city without exciting comment," Fox said.

"Of course." Kouradin closed his eyes. "Somebody ordinary. Somebody respectable. Somebody with a beard. Somebody with long hair, so we could use a wig." His eyes popped open. "A RABBI!" he squealed, clapping his hands.

Fox contemplated me thoughtfully. "Not bad, Kouradin, not bad at all. Well, Moretti, how do you feel about becoming the only Irish-Italian Jew in New York City?"

"It's a distinction I never thought to attain," I replied.

Fox told Kouradin to return with the necessary make-up and costumes as quickly as possible and not to mention the purpose of them to anyone, on pain of instant dismissal. Kouradin left at a rapid trot, and Fox occupied the twenty-five minutes until his return with reading and editing the manuscripts written by the inhabitants of the locked room.

When the theatrical reporter re-entered, he had a large wrapped bundle under his arm. He tapped it with satisfaction. "From Tony Pastor's. They have an excellent costume room, and the costume mistress is a very dear friend of mine."

"Open it up," Fox ordered.

The bundle contained a worn and rusty black suit, scuffed black shoes badly run down at the heels, a flat, wide-brimmed black hat, a black full beard, and a black, curly wig. Fox picked up the wig. "That's a woman's wig," he said.

Kouradin spread his expressive hands. "With the hat and the beard, who can tell?"

I removed my suit and put on the black clothes, which fitted me tolerably well. The shoes were tight, but wearable. "What about a black tie?" I asked. Kouradin explained that the beard made one unnecessary. He fitted the wig down over my head and adjusted the black hat over it. Then he held the beard up against my face and stepped back to study the result. "What do you think, Mr. Fox?"

"Excellent. Apply your spirit gum, Kouradin."

When the beard had been secured to my face, the theatrical reporter produced his two final touches, a pair of wire-rimmed eyeglasses with plate-glass lenses and a Jewish-language newspaper. I put the eyeglasses on my nose and slipped the newspaper into my side pocket. "Rosh Hashanah. Oy gevult. Bar mitzva. Mazel tof. How's that?"

"Just try not to talk, Moretti, and you may make it." Fox clapped me on the back and propelled me toward the door. "Walk with a shuffle and keep bent over, as if you've spent most of your life reading the Torah. I'll keep your clothes here, so you can pick them up when you bring me your story. Go to the end of the hall and take the backstairs. Good luck and Godspeed!"

"Mr. Fox," I protested, "I don't even have money for carfare!"

He sighed, tucked a dollar bill in my pocket, and closed the door firmly behind me.

9

A Manhattan Odyssey

BY THE TIME I reached the street, I was stooping and shuffling very well, I thought. My hands, however, felt they should be contributing more to the impersonation, so I occupied them with passing the newspaper back and forth. I kept my eyes fixed on a spot on the sidewalk ten feet in front of me and moved my lips as if mumbling prayers. Actually, I was reciting "The Kerry Recruit."

I resisted the strong temptation to turn and study the faces of the pedestrians behind me, searching for Sharkey and his fat friend, or for Tomaso and Gaetano. After a moment's reflection I continued on my shuffling way. I couldn't pick and choose between my followers, I realized—if I hoped to lose the threatening ones, I must also resign myself to losing my protectors.

I walked along Dover Street toward City Hall Park. As I crossed Park Row I saw my first policeman, a red-faced patrolman whose Irish features were vaguely familiar to me. His eyes met mine and hesitated a moment. I had a sudden impulse to make the sign of the cross but suppressed it in time. His eyes moved on, and in a moment he was behind me, and I was on the sidewalk heading toward City Hall.

Traversing that short length of sidewalk was like running a gauntlet. Not only were there more policemen, in and out of uniform, than I had seen in any one place since May Day; there were lawyers, judges, ward heelers, newspapermen, and unjailed criminals of high and low degree, the majority of whom were known to me by face if not by name. In the hundred yards I shuffled to the door of City Hall, I passed a prosecutor who had once told me I deserved to be behind bars, a police reporter who owed me thirty dollars, a burglar who had often drunk with me at McSorley's, a playboy who had once tried to eject me from a private party at Harry Hill's Rendezvous of Champions on Houston Street, and a bail bondsman who had been professionally valuable to me on more than one occasion. My heart was in my throat every step of the way as I awaited the inevitable "Why, Moretti! Come out from behind that beard, you scoundrel, and take your medicine!"

Somehow I arrived at the door unrecognized and entered gratefully into the gloomy hallway with its ineradicable smell of steam heat and stale air and poverty. I had searched for titles before and knew where to go to investigate the ownership of the Circus. The dusty volume that listed the properties on Eighteenth Street between Eighth and Ninth avenues told me that the building that housed Axel Klepp's bordello was owned in trust by the Chelsea Fidelity Bank and Trust Company, with an address on West 23rd Street.

I left City Hall and caught the Broadway car north. A large woman with a shopping bag sat down beside me and said, *"Gut morgn. Vos makht ir?"* Before she could go any further I touched my lips, shook my head, and shrugged my shoulders helplessly. She expressed her deep sympathy for my affliction by patting my knee and entertaining me with an utterly incomprehensible Yiddish monologue for twenty blocks. Every so often she paused for breath, and I tried to adopt the appropriate facial expression. Apparently I was not entirely successful, for by the time I struggled around her bulk at 23rd Street, she was regarding me with an expression of growing uneasiness.

As I walked to the bank, I thought about how to get the information I wanted. I doubted whether a West Side banker would have much familiarity with rabbis, so I was not uneasy about any minor flaws in my characterization. Bank employees were, however, notoriously close-mouthed about the affairs of their clients. What story could I tell that would persuade a suspicious financial watchdog to release a bone of financial information?

I entered the bank lobby and approached a guard. I bobbed my head and said, "I would like to speak to one of your trust officers, please." He gave me a hard look. "What about?" he demanded. "I would like to pay him some money," I said. He pursed his lips judiciously, as if considering the bestowal of a great boon. "Over there," he said with a jerk of his head. "Second desk from the wall."

The executive to whom he directed me was thin-faced and sharp-featured, with colorless hair carefully combed over a large bald spot. He was wearing a suit that smelled of cleaning fluid. He looked at me coldly and made no move to rise. "My name is Jason Prettyman," he said, in a voice that suggested a nasal obstruction. "May I help you?"

"Thank you, Mr. Prettyman. I am Rabbi Marx. I'm here to settle for the family of little Rivke Schindler with the gentleman who owns the building on Eighteenth Street, and it's a great pleasure, I tell you." I smiled broadly to indicate great pleasure. "I look forward to shaking his hand."

Prettyman frowned. "I'm sorry, Rabbi Marx, but I don't understand what you mean. What is it you want from us?"

"Why, the gentleman's name!" I said in surprise. "How can I pay him back the money if I don't know his name? He doesn't live in the building any more. How can I find him without a name?"

Prettyman began tapping his desk with his fingertips. "What man, Rabbi? What money? What building? I don't know what you're talking about."

"Of course you don't. Excuse me, Mr. Prettyman, I'm sorry." I smiled humbly. "Allow me to explain from the beginning. The

Schindlers, Morris and Sarah, are members of our temple— or *were* members, I should say, since they live in Buffalo at present. Before they moved, they lived on Eighteenth Street—but that was *East* Eighteenth Street, you understand. But how could a little greenhorn fresh off the boat understand the difference?"

As Prettyman continued tapping I spun my story—how little Rivke Schindler had stayed on in the Old Country, living with her grandparents, while her mother and father had begun a new life in the land of opportunity. How, after both grandparents had died, Rivke's relatives had bought her a ticket to New York City, and she had arrived with two addresses— one on East Eighteenth Street, where her parents no longer lived, and the other in Buffalo, which she had neither the information nor the funds to reach. And how little Rivke, hoping to find sympathetic ex-neighbors who would help reunite her with her parents, made her way to an address on Eighteenth Street, but on the wrong side of the city. "It was *West* Eighteenth Street, and there wasn't a person within two miles who had ever heard of the Schindlers! Imagine what might have happened to little Rivke except for that kind gentleman!"

"The gentleman who lived in the house on West Eighteenth Street," Prettyman said.

"The gentleman who *owns* the house on West Eighteenth Street," I corrected. "He mentioned to Rivke that he owned the building. That's how I will be able to find him."

Prettyman stopped tapping his fingers and began playing with a letter opener. "And this gentleman helped the little girl reach her parents?" he asked.

"He took her to the station, bought her a ticket to Buffalo, and sent her father a telegram saying she was on her way! And can you imagine, he was so modest, he didn't even sign his name! He just put down 'A friend.' "

"He certainly was a good samaritan," Prettyman said with a hint of distaste. "Very well, Rabbi, I guess I understand all that. But I still don't see what you want from us."

"It took Morris Schindler three months to save the money to repay the gentleman. Then he sent it to me and asked me to take care of it. But when I went to the address on West Eighteenth Street, the gentleman had moved. There was nobody there that knew where to find him. So I went to City Hall to find the name of the owner of the building. There I find the building is listed as held in trust by this bank." I smiled ingratiatingly and told him the address. "So if you'll be so good as to look up the trust and tell me whose name is on it, I'll see that the Schindler's debt is repaid, Mr. Prettyman."

The bank officer regarded me silently for at least ten seconds. Then he said, "You are asking me to look up a blind trust and tell you who set it up, Rabbi?" I nodded with an expression of simple-minded confidence. He continued, "You know, of course, that the purpose of setting up blind trusts in the first place is to protect the identity of the property owner?"

"But not from one who only wants to pay back money, surely!" I spread my hands persuasively. "Why would the property owner object to that? I'd be grateful—wouldn't you?"

Mr. Prettyman regarded me a few seconds more and then rose from his chair. "If you'll excuse me a moment, Rabbi, I need to check something. You just wait right here." He walked around his desk and started across the lobby. I thought he was heading for a door marked Trusts until he approached the bank guard and began speaking rapidly to him. The guard glanced in my direction and then looked away. He answered briefly, and Prettyman made a decisive gesture with his hand.

I headed for the street door.

Prettyman saw me first and cried a warning to the guard. The guard turned toward me and started to head me off. I began to trot and the guard began to trot. Prettyman called "Stop that man!" and scurried toward me in the guard's wake, no doubt dreaming of commendations and rewards. I began to run. The guard began to run.

At that moment a man of ample girth and capitalistic appearance entered the bank from the street. He had barely enough time to register startled disapproval with his porcine eyes when I caromed off his belly and struck the doorjamb with my shoulder. I rebounded against his side, sending him lurching into the bank guard, whose feet shot out from under him. He sat down heavily on the floor. The man of girth thrust out his gold-headed cane in an attempt to keep his balance, and its shaft slipped between Mr. Prettyman's pumping legs, sending him stumbling on top of the guard. The capitalist, his balance still upset, crashed down on both of them.

This moment of deliverance gave me time to slip through the door and out onto Twenty-third Street. I turned and hurried along the crowded sidewalk toward Ninth Avenue. I was thirty feet from the bank entrance when I heard the voice of Prettyman behind me shouting, "The man with the beard! Stop him!" I doubled my speed, moving as fast as possible without breaking into a run, and wove my way between the pedestrians who thronged the walk. One or two glanced at me curiously, but with the blessed neutralism of the New Yorker took no action to arrest my flight. By the time I reached the Ninth Avenue elevated line I was confident I had outdistanced my pursuers.

I ascended to the platform and awaited a southbound train, being careful to keep other travelers between myself and the stairways. As I waited I considered my next move.

Well, so much for the easy way, I thought. *It's into the cannon's mouth, my son.*

The steam engine pulled in with a whoosh and a roar. I found an empty seat in the third car and, concealed behind my newspaper, avoided conversation until I left the train at Canal Street. I walked east, crossing West Broadway and Broadway, and turned left at Lafayette. A block north lay Hester Street.

It took me more than two hours to find the tenement where Maisie Goertz's family lived, and an hour beyond that before I was talking to Maisie's little sister Bunny. I tracked her down in an areaway between Grand and Broome streets. She was dressed in a hand-me-down dress and cracked shoes. Her pale face, with its large yellow eyes and pointed chin, was as trustworthy as a fox's.

"Yaa, whiskers, whatcha want?" she demanded truculently. "You want a girl? How much you pay, whiskers?"

I told her I was a friend of her sister's, and I needed her help. Her face lit up. "Hey, you're from the Circus? Maisie's changed her mind? Okay, when do they want me? Tonight?" She bounced up and down on her toes impatiently.

"No, of course they don't want you!" I said indignantly. "Good God! A ten-year-old child! Do you have any idea what kind of a place the Circus is?"

"Whaddya think, I'm just off the farm? Course I have!" She put one hand on her skinny hip and twitched her body, looking up at me from under lowered lids. "I'll be selling what they want to buy," she said huskily.

It took me a few moments to regain the power of speech. Then I said carefully, "It's a great temptation I'm fighting to let me hand follow its inclination and give you the spanking of your young life."

She inspected me, frowning. "You talk funny for a Hebe."

"And you talk terrible for anybody! You sound like you haven't any morals at all! Now listen—the Circus is one of the worst places in the world, do you understand? Women who work there are exploited, degraded, sacrificed to the brute lusts of men who are worse than animals! You'd be better off in jail or on the poor farm!"

She scratched her head and then cleaned her fingernail with her sharp little teeth. "You sound like a Mick. How come you're dressed up like a Hebe?"

"It's a long story, Bunny. What I said was the truth; I am a friend of your sister, and I do need your help. And you're right about me not being a rabbi, too. My name's Paddy Moretti, and

I work for a horse-race newspaper, and the police are looking for me to put me in jail. The only way I can save myself is if you get a message to your sister at the Circus for me."

Her yellow eyes narrowed. "They got a reward out for you?"

Not wishing to put our relationship under too great a strain at the outset, I assured her there wasn't a penny to be gained from my apprehension. She looked disappointed, but still open-minded. "What kind of message?" she asked.

"You've got to tell her to unlock the side door for me so I can get in tonight without being seen. Tell her I've got to get into Axel Klepp's office and go through his records—it's the only chance I've got to keep the police from convicting her friend Marya Perlman of murder."

Bunny's eyes widened. "Marya Perlman? Are you a friend of Marya Perlman too?"

I nodded. "A very good friend."

She grinned. "Yeah, I bet. Marya's got a lot of good friends. Maisie says if she'd start selling it she'd make a mint."

I felt myself flush under my false beard. "My right hand is getting this terrible itch, and I don't know how long I can keep it away from you," I warned. "Now pay attention. Tell her the police have arrested Marya and they'll hang her for sure unless I can find evidence that points to someone else. Tell her I'll be coming to the side door after two o'clock tomorrow morning—"

"You better make it later than that," Bunny said. "Things are really going good at two. You better make it three, anyway."

"All right, three then. Tell her just to leave the lock off—I know how to get to Klepp's office. Can you get her that message today, Bunny?"

She nodded vigorously. "Sure, I can get in any time I want. I know everybody there. They're all friends of mine. Someday—"

"Someday," I interrupted, "you'll have this fine young husband whose right hand will also have this unbearable itch. Good God, child, hasn't your sister told you how much she hates the life there?"

Her face became solemn. "Yeah. I know she don't like it. Sometimes they beat her up. And they make her work when she's sick. And some of the johns are really bughouse. But it don't have to be that way."

"It doesn't?"

"Of course not! Once you learn the ropes, you can meet some rich society swell, and he'll put you in your own flat on Fifth Avenue, and you'll have a maid, and wear fur coats, and drink French champagne, and eat chicken or beefsteak or anything you want!" She tilted her head and closed her eyes. "And you can go to plays and operas, and ride on sailboats, and have fifty different pairs of shoes, and if you don't like somebody, you can just spit in his eye!"

"All that, just for learning the ropes?" I asked.

"Sure! And then when you get tired of it, you find yourself a duke or an earl to marry, and live in a great big mansion in the country!"

"And have children?"

She opened her eyes in surprise. "Yeah, I guess so, if you want to." Her expression indicated her inability to understand why anyone would want to. "Anyway, that's the way it's gonna be, just as soon as I can learn the ropes!"

"If you say so, Bunny." I dug in my pocket and produced the change from the dollar Richard K. Fox had given me. I selected a quarter and handed it to the child. "Here," I said. "For your fur coat and French champagne fund."

She bit the coin and then slipped it into her dress pocket. "Thanks. And if I was you, I wouldn't count on them whiskers to fool the coppers. They're strictly the phonus bolonus."

"I'll bear your words in mind. Good-by, Bunny."

I left her in the areaway and walked to Broome Street. From there it was only two blocks to the butcher shop where Sasha had told me I could leave a message for him.

The butcher, Karl, was a fat man with an absolutely hairless face. He looked at me suspiciously from watery eyes and denied knowing anyone named Sasha. "That's not his real name," I said. "His real name is—" I paused as I thought back to my first meeting with Marya and her friends in Zum Groben Michel. "—Felix Algauer," I remembered aloud. "Marya Perlman calls him Sasha because she says he looks like a Sasha."

Karl's watery eyes widened in alarm, and he bent over his butcher's block and began brushing away imaginary scraps of meat. "*Ach, Gott,* don't say her name out loud! Police spies are everywhere!" he whispered harshly. "Who are you?"

"A friend of Marya's. My name is Moretti. I work for a newspaper."

"A newspaper!" he echoed. "You want to write about Marya in a newspaper?"

"No, no, it's not that kind of newspaper. It's a sporting paper, a horse race paper. No, I'm a friend of Marya's, that's all. I'm trying to help her."

"You are not a comrade. I have never seen you at any meetings."

"That's right. I don't go to meetings. Look, Sasha said you could get a message to him. Can you?"

A woman carrying a market basket entered. "Later," the butcher hissed. "*Ja,* Mrs. Koppelmeyer. *Guten tag.* What would you like today?"

The woman poked at a goose, sniffed at a pork roast, squeezed a hare, and finally departed with a pound of Braunschweiger. When the door closed behind her Karl wiped his soft white hands on a dirty towel. "You want me to get a message to Felix? I say I do not know anyone named Felix. But if I did, what message would it be?"

I leaned closer to him. "Tell him tonight I'm going to a whorehouse called the Circus on Eighteenth Street. I'm looking for evidence that could help to clear Marya of killing Tim Kanady— it's a long shot, but it's the only one I have. Have you got that?"

He licked his lips and repeated, "Whorehouse . . . Circus . . . Eighteenth Street . . . looking for evidence."

"And tell him they don't like me in there. Tell him I'm going in at three A.M., and if I'm not out by five, it's because somebody doesn't want me to leave. Tell him that I will be indebted for any help he can give me."

The butcher looked down at his chopping block and scratched at a dried bloodstain. "I don't know," he mumbled. "How can I promise? Whorehouses—killings? I'm a family man, I have a business to run—"

I put my face close to his. "Just do it." I grated. "It's for Marya, comrade. What would Felix do to you if he found out you wouldn't help Marya?"

Karl looked up at me and his eyes were wide with panic. "You wouldn't—" he began.

"Wouldn't I?"

The door opened and another customer entered. Karl glanced from her to me and then back to her in uncertainty, obviously equally uneasy at the prospect of leaving our conversation unresolved and of continuing it in the customer's presence. I solved his problem for him. "You'll tell him, Karl? *Danke schön*—I'll count on it. I would hate to be disappointed. *Auf Wiedersehen*, Karl," I gave a little bow to the new customer and left the shop.

I paused on the crowded sidewalk outside to consider my next move. It was a long time until 3:00 A.M. Where could I spend it safely? Obviously I couldn't continue walking the streets, even if my sore feet would allow it. I suspected that Bunny Goertz was correct about the amount of protection I could count on from my false beard. Where could a wanted man with less than a dollar in his pocket go to spend a safe and comfortable twelve hours in Manhattan?

I began to walk west. Overhead the sky had turned gray, and a damp wind blew along the street. I could almost taste the coming rain. *Damn, what happens to spirit gum and crepe hair when it rains?* I wondered.

I didn't realize where I was headed until I found myself turning south from Broome onto Lafayette, going toward Chambers

Street. Of course—*The Spirit of the Times* office! Even if I couldn't risk entering the office myself, I could still get a message to my fellow workers, and someone could pass me out a key and an address to a room where I could spend the day and evening in safety!

I rounded the corner into Chambers Street. *The Spirit of the Times* building was in the next block. Halfway there I spied Blinky, the blind pencil-and-shoelace vendor, leaning against the wall by the entrance.

My spirits zoomed upward. All I had to do was whisper my needs to Blinky as I passed him, and he would forward the message to the next staff member who entered the newspaper office. Then my colleagues in the editorial room could decide where to direct me for my safe harbor and send the key and address down to Blinky on the sidewalk outside, where I would receive them from him as I finished my walk around the block.

I started across the street and then had to leap back on the curb as a produce wagon rattled by. After it came a fashionable barouche, then a wagonette with eight passengers on a sightseeing tour. As I waited for the traffic to clear, I happened to glance along the other side of Chambers Street.

Standing just inside a doorway directly across the street from Blinky was a broad-shouldered man in a yellow and black checked suit. Although he held an opened newspaper in front of him, his eyes were fixed on the doorway of *The Spirit of the Times*. It was Sharkey, and I knew that my false whiskers wouldn't fool him for an instant.

I stood frozen on the curb, considering my next action. I couldn't continue on down Chambers Street, obviously. There was a back entrance to the newspaper building, but if Axel Klepp was having the front door watched, he was likely to have a man in the back also, perhaps the fat man in the too-tight suit whom I had last met behind the clubhouse at Gravesend. The possibility of meeting him again in an alley was uninviting.

A man jostled me from behind and swore. I realized I couldn't keep standing on the curb obstructing traffic indefinitely. Confident that Sharkey had not noticed my approach, I turned down the side street to put a square block of masonry between us. Then I headed south again.

I walked all the way to the Battery without thinking of any safe place to take my aching feet. *Ah, Moretti, you've used up all Manhattan,* I thought, *and now there's only one place to go.* I boarded the Staten Island ferry, and sank down on a bench with a groan of relief.

I fell asleep on the ride across, and I awoke to the babble and bustle of the passengers leaving the boat in the borough of Richmond. I joined them automatically, and it was only when I was ashore that I realized I had absolutely nothing to do on Staten Island. So I turned around, paid another fare, and got back aboard.

I went back and forth between Manhattan and Staten Island for six hours. As the afternoon wore on, the wind rose and the sky darkened, and whitecaps appeared on the sea. Huge drops of rain began spattering the open deck of the ferry, and many passengers, including me, found it impossible to find shelter. I unfolded my newspaper and hunched beneath it on my bench. It was impossible to keep from getting wet.

A man and his wife and their small child were sharing my bench with me. As the rain increased in severity, the man rummaged through the canvas bag he was carrying and produced a piece of oilcloth six feet square, which he unfolded to use as a tent for his family. I regarded them enviously as my sodden newspaper dripped streams of water down my beard.

The woman said something to her husband, and he smiled and nodded. Turning to me, he spoke courteously in Yiddish and gestured to indicate there was room for me under the oilcloth. I touched my lips, shook my head, and shrugged pathetically, as I had done on the Broadway car earlier, and crowded under the improvised tent.

The woman was sitting beside me with her child on her lap,

and her husband at the other end of the bench. Our heads were all close together. As the rain beat down on the oilcloth, the woman rattled on at a great rate, and I nodded and smiled as if I had some foggy idea of what she was talking about. The child, who was a boy of two or two and a half, regarded me fixedly. He had dark brown eyes with heavy lashes, a tiny nose with a drop at the end of it, and a small, fat mouth that hung open. I began to get uneasy under his unblinking attention and turned my face away from him.

The ferry's engines stopped and then reversed, indicating that we were pulling into the Manhattan slip. Passengers crowded toward the bow. The man said something to me and began to fold his oilcloth. The woman added some pleasantries of her own and bounced the child. I nodded, smiled, and started to rise.

And then disaster struck.

The child reached out his chubby fists, secured his fingers in my beard, and peeled me like a banana.

The woman stared as though she was a witness to the desecration of a temple, and her husband barked an exclamation of incredulity. I seized the soggy whiskers and attempted to wrest them from the child's fists. He hung on with the strength of the infant Hercules strangling the serpent in his crib. He also began to wail piteously. I cursed under my breath and pulled harder, and the child began to rise in the air. His mother gave a shriek and clutched him to her bosom. His father grabbed at my shoulder.

Passengers were staring at us, and one man seemed about ready to join our little group. I gave a desperate tug to the crepe hair, and the mother gave a hearty pull to the child. The father began to wrap one arm around my neck. I realized that in another few seconds I would become the object of considerable attention, probably some of it official.

I released the beard and ran.

The man who had been approaching put out an arm to stop me, but I sidestepped him and slipped into the crowd of disembarking passengers at the bow. I thought I could hear shouts behind me, but in a few moments, I was off the boat and walking rapidly through the terminal.

Apparently I was safe, but I felt as naked as a plucked chicken. My rabbi's costume, with its wide black hat, rusty black suit, and flowing curls, cried out for the lost beard; it seemed to me that every passer-by must realize I was an imposter. And now the fact that I had no necktie was obvious to all.

Outside, darkness had fallen over the city. The street lights threw down islands of danger on the sidewalks, through which I hurried with my shoulders hunched and my head half-buried in my turned-up collar. I stayed well to the east of City Hall and the newspaper office, and soon I was moving among the drunks, derelicts, and degenerates who made their home on the Bowery. The street was charged with its regular nocturnal energy, so different from the lassitude and despair that lay over it like dirty snow during the days. I passed Bannerman's Natural Science Museum, where a barker on a raised platform pointed out the wonders of the Turtle Boy to a small group of "slummers" in evening clothes; the Turtle Boy was a young man with lost, unfocused eyes, dressed in short trousers and a sleeveless shirt, sitting on a very low stool. His arms and legs, barely half normal length, ended in fleshy white flippers. As the barker talked, a gentleman in the audience leaned forward and rapped one of the flippers with his cane. The Turtle Boy jerked away, wincing with pain.

"Think he's wearing some kind of gloves, do you, sir?" the barker cried. "Then come up and shake his hand! See for yourself whether them flippers of his ain't good firm flesh just like your own! Come on up and shake hands with the Turtle Boy, sir! You can tell your friends about it for years!"

The gentleman's companions, male and female, urged him forward with dares and laughter. He held back, shaking his head in embarrassment. "No, no, can't do that," he argued. "Might get some awful disease!"

I moved along the sidewalk, past the posters advertising the giant and dwarf, the fat lady and the tattooed man, the half-man-half-woman, and the human pincushion. I escaped from the bright lights outside the freak museum only to be trapped under a street light outside a ten-cent-a-night lodging house. "Moretti, is that you?" called a loud voice.

I leaped as if someone had dropped ice down my neck. I recognized the speaker; it was the gray-faced reporter with the bloodshot eyes who had shared my weekend sanctuary at the *Police Gazette*—Settlemeyer was his name. Pinned under the street light like a butterfly in a specimen case, I acknowledged the greeting. Settlemeyer threw one arm around my shoulders. He was by no means sober. "Moretti, you dago mick, what the hell are you doing on the Bowery? Looking for a good wild-card poker game?" He struck me lightly on the biceps. "How 'bout a little seven-card high-low with deuces and treys wild? You're hell on wheels on that one, boy." He laughed foolishly.

I tried to edge away from him. "It's me fondest wish in the world, but I'll have to take a rain check," I said. "The press of business, unfortunately. Nice to have seen you."

His arm tightened. "Wait a minute! Don't go running off into the night! Lets us have a drink and talk it over." He began to draw me along the sidewalk toward a saloon a few doors down. "Like to get to know you better, Moretti. Interesting fellow. We can talk about horse racing."

A police officer was thirty or forty feet away and approaching us. We would meet, I calculated in panic, immediately in front of the saloon's front window, which threw a cheery glow onto the sidewalk. I leaned back on my heels. "Can't do it, me boyo, much as I'd like to. We'll make it one day soon, though. And the drinks'll be on me. Count on it."

I tried to slide out of his grasp, but he hung on like a limpet. "Come on, Moretti!" he insisted loudly. "What's the matter? You take the pledge or something?"

The policeman couldn't have been more than twenty feet away, and my name must have been audible to him. Clearly, I couldn't wait any longer. "Sorry, Settlemeyer," I said, and then twisted toward him and dropped below his arm, simultaneously shoving him toward the nearest wall. He stumbled back, lost his balance, and sprawled on the sidewalk. Looking up at me incredulously, he cried "Moretti! What are you doing? That's a hell of a way to treat a friend, Moretti!"

I walked away from him rapidly, not daring to look over my shoulder to see if the policeman was giving chase. Behind me I could hear Settlemeyer's remonstrances, and he mentioned my name twice more before the rattling roar of an elevated train overhead drowned him out.

I turned a corner into a crowded side street where a number of sailors were engaged in spirited negotiation with three ladies of the evening. "A *dollar?*" cried one of the tars indignantly. "You think you're Lillian Russell and I'm Diamond Jim?" I swung around them and put them between me and my possible pursuer. One of the women clutched at my arm as I passed. "How about it, handsome?" she asked in a rasping voice. "Only a dollar for a trip to the Promised Land." I mumbled a polite refusal and shook loose, hurrying along the busy walk. I glanced over my shoulder in time to see the policeman pass the corner and continue his beat along the Bowery.

I gave a sigh of relief. I was suddenly overwhelmingly tired, so exhausted I felt unable to walk any farther. I leaned against the wall of a brick building and let myself slide down it until I was sitting on the sidewalk with my legs thrust out before me. After a moment I crossed them tailor-fashion so they wouldn't be stepped on by passing pedestrians. I put my head back against the wall and closed my eyes. Since the brim of my hat pressed uncomfortably against the back of my neck, I took it off and dropped it on the sidewalk beside me, brim upward.

A few moments later I opened my eyes to find a gentleman in evening clothes swaying over me. "Unhappy man," he said owlishly, "see what your addiction to demon rum has done to you! Wine is a mocker, and strong drink is raging! Take the

advice of a good Shamaritan before it's too late—put the cursh
of John Barleycorn behind you, and regain your rightful place
in society." He fumbled in his pocket for his billfold and withdrew a bill from it. "God marks the shparrow in his fall," he
said, and dropped the bill into my hat.

Another gentleman in white tie tugged at his arm and said,
"Come on, Nickie, can't keep the ladies waiting."

The first gentleman turned to his friend and explained, "No
one is lost to shalvation, Waldo. We're all our brother's keeper,
remember. Let him who is without sin casht the first stone. Right?"

"Right," said Waldo.

"All right then—let's go get our ashes hauled." The two gentlemen, arm in arm, continued their unsteady way down the
sidewalk. I picked up the bill from my hat and held it so I could
read the denomination. It was a five.

Before I could put it in my pocket, however, a hand like a
condor's talons closed over my wrist. I turned to look into the
eyes of a man whose head was on the level of my own. An expression of indescribable ferocity convulsed his features as he
said, "Hand it over, before I pull your guts out of your mouth
and strangle you with them."

He was a man with huge shoulders, a deep chest, and a neck
like a log, who must have stood over six feet when he had legs
to stand on. He had no legs, however; his massive torso, supported on three-inch stumps, rested upon a wooden dolly. The
hand that was not crushing my wrist lay flat on the pavement
to provide locomotion. There was a tin cup hanging on his chest,
suspended by a cord around his neck.

"Hand it over? The money? It's the money you're asking for?"
I procrastinated. His fingers increased their pressure, and I
thought I heard my wrist bones creak. "Oh, the *money*!" I cried,
waving the bill in the air. "Of course! Take it!" He plucked the
bill from my fingers and eased the pressure slightly.

He thrust the money into his shirt pocket without looking at
it. "You trying to cut into my territory? Who told you you could

set up here? I ought to break your goddamn hands!" he growled, baring the few rotted teeth that remained in his gums. "Come here!" He tightened his grip on my wrist again and, at the same time, grasped my neck with his other hand, dragging my head down against his hard belly. The ammoniac smell of urine was overpowering. "You want me to run my wheels over your fingers? Next time I will! You think I can't?" He jerked my hand down under the dolly and held it against the sidewalk as he released my head and propelled himself forward with his other hand. I felt the sharp edge of the iron wheel press against my knuckles and begin to crush them. I cried out in pain. The wheel stopped. "Next time!" the cripple whispered harshly. "Now get out of here!"

I struggled to my feet. It seemed incredible that passers-by were walking and talking within a few feet of us, paying no more attention to us than to the trash in the gutters. I flexed my fingers to assure myself they were still in working order, resettled my wig on my head, and buttoned my jacket. I glanced down at the man on the dolly, but he was staring straight ahead, apparently oblivious to me.

I walked slowly along the sidewalk, keeping to the shadows as much as possible. *My God, I can't even sit down for a moment's rest*, I thought. I felt as if I were tottering, likely to stumble and fall at any moment. I crossed a street, hearing the shouted curses of a wagon driver who almost ran me down. It was hard to lift my foot to step up to the curb.

Dully I wondered what time it was. Perhaps ten o'clock, perhaps ten-thirty, certainly no later than eleven. And the earliest I could safely get to the Circus was three in the morning—that was the hour Bunny Goertz had given me, and the hour I had passed on to Sasha. *And me ready to fall down on the spot, and without a half-dollar to my name—where can I spend four hours?*

I was in front of a building with its windows painted black when a door opened, and a figure emerged and banished all feeling of fatigue from my body. As I stiffened in recognition, the light from behind his short, twisted body fell across my face. He stopped on the threshold and stared up at me in astonishment.

It was the hunchback who had brought Sharkey to get me the night I had visited the Circus.

For a moment we both stood frozen. Then, as he drew away and opened his mouth, I put my foot against his pouter-pigeon chest and pushed as hard as I could. He sailed back as if he had been shot from a gun and ended his flight against a table fifteen feet inside the room, amid a welter of broken glass, screaming women, and cursing men. I pivoted and began running along the dark sidewalk toward the nearest alley. I reached it just as the sounds of pursuit arose behind me.

I ran down the alley until I tripped and fell. The blackness was absolute. I crawled on on my hands and knees. My heart was pounding so loudly I could hardly hear the street noises behind me. My fingers scrambled across unmentionable filth. Pounding feet thudded along the sidewalk and passed the alley entrance and diminished in the distance. My arms gave out, and I collapsed on my face in the darkness.

I must have lain in the alley for ten or fifteen minutes, only half-conscious, until I felt the touch of something wispy and delicate against my cheek. I raised my head and opened my eyes, which by now had accommodated to the blackness.

A rat as large as a terrier was sniffing at me from three inches away.

I gagged in disgust and swung at the creature with one hand. It leaped aside and struck at my arm, its teeth grazing my flesh. My hand found a broken fragment of brick, and I tried to smash the rat with it. It sidestepped easily and drew away from me toward an overturned refuse can, where I now saw a half-dozen of its fellows waiting and regarding me unblinkingly.

I rose to my knees. Something that looked like a dead curly-haired animal lay on the ground in front of me. I realized it was my wig, and picked it up and adjusted it on my head. Its lining felt wet and slippery. The rats watched me as I climbed to my feet. "Don't let me disturb you, boys," I said aloud, backing away from them toward the mouth of the alley. "*Bon appetit*," I giggled inanely as I stumbled backwards.

Reaching the street, I leaned against the side of a building and closed my eyes. Where could I go? I simply could not continue to totter purposelessly around the Bowery for four more hours. If I didn't find a place off the street, it was only a matter of time until I either collapsed or was attacked or apprehended. I couldn't sit down against a building without being rousted by a panhandler. I couldn't hide in an alley without being gnawed by rats. There were people who knew me on the streets, people who were searching for me. I didn't have enough money to sit drinking in a dark barroom—

And then I remembered. *The Velvet Room! The Velvet Room at Crapaud's!* It was not more than a block away, it only cost a quarter, it was as dark as the bottom of a mine, and once I was inside nobody would know whether I lived or died till sunrise! The Velvet Room, of course! Why hadn't I thought of it before?

I began to walk along the sidewalk, concentrating on moving as inconspicuously as possible. I rounded the corner and saw the sign reading "CRAPAUD'S" halfway down the block. When I looked down at my feet, they appeared to be unusually far away, and I wasn't sure of my control over them. The sidewalk was crowded with people who swam across my vision like fish in a tank, disappearing from the periphery of my sight as though swallowed up in black water. For many moments I seemed to draw no closer to the sign, and then suddenly I was standing below it. I opened the door and stepped inside.

The front room at Crapaud's was smoky and noisy, and smelled as corrupt as a rotten egg. The middle of the room was filled with tables, most of them occupied by women who were drinking on percentage and the men who paid for the privilege of pawing them. To the left was a long bar crowded with patrons attracted more by the price of drinks than by feminine allure—

Crapaud's charged fifteen cents for a two-ounce shot of whiskey, twenty-five cents for a double. Most of the men wore working clothes, but here and there in the line of bent backs was a tuxedo jacket or black tailcoat.

To my right, halfway along the wall, was a doorway covered with a black velvet curtain. A man sat in a chair beside it, his arms crossed and his feet hooked around the legs of the chair. He had a face that reminded me of drawings of the great carved heads on Easter Island—hollow eye sockets, a long scoop of a nose, and heavy, cruel lips curving down over a massive jaw. He glanced up indifferently as I approached.

I found a quarter in my pocket and handed it to him. He tried to gouge it with his thumbnail before slipping it into the pocket of his open vest. "You're here early," he said, in a harsh voice that suggested damaged vocal chords.

I nodded without answering. I stood with my head down and my eyes on the floor, hoping to avoid giving him any detail about me to remember. I could feel his gaze on me for a moment before he said, "All right, go on in. Tubbo will take care of you." He drew the curtain back for me, and I stepped through the doorway.

I had never been in a Velvet Room before, although I had heard about them for years. There were a half-dozen or more in the Bowery area, of which Crapaud's was perhaps the best known. They all offered the same service: a dark, quiet room where a drunk could "finish off the night" with a bowl of straight alcohol for a quarter. And they all enjoyed the same unsavory reputation; not everyone who entered a Velvet Room, it was said, exited from it under his own power the following morning.

When the velvet curtain fell behind me, I felt as if I were suddenly almost deaf and totally blind. The sounds from the barroom were muffled and distant and the blackness around me was impenetrable. The air was warm and heavy, and the corrupt smell of the outer room was mixed with an odor of sickening sweetness, like a surfeit of gardenias, which I took to be opium.

I raised my arms and extended them in front of me and to both sides. They touched nothing. I took one very careful step into the room, and then a second. Still my fingers touched nothing. I reached behind me, hoping for the reassurance of the velvet drape, but I had come too far into the room, and my hand encountered only air. I felt as lonely as a shipwreck sailor on an empty sea.

I was unable to move. Every direction seemed as perilous as every other. I was no longer sure the entrance *was* behind me— perhaps I had turned as I stepped into the room, and the velvet drape was to my right or left. Whatever moral stamina I had begun the day with seemed to have drained from me. My teeth began to chatter, and a sudden chill brought gooseflesh to my thighs.

A hand touched my arm, and I started violently. The fingers felt large and soft, and their squeeze was gently suggestive. "Just come with me, now," a voice murmured close to my ear. "We'll just find you a nice place to sit down, that's a boy."

My invisible guide led me forward in the darkness. After half a dozen steps, his voice whispered, "Here you are, lambkins. You just sit yourself down and I'll have you a bowl of something good in a jiffy." The soft fingers pressed against my shoulders, and I allowed myself to be directed into a chair. I felt a table top in front of me, the surface rough and sticky.

After a few moments, I became aware of gradations in the darkness. In the direction of the sounds from the barroom, there was a hairline of light, which must mark the bottom of the velvet curtain. To my left and right, if I didn't look directly at them, were shapes of slightly lighter dark than the surrounding areas. My hands on the table before me seemed on the verge of visibility.

Someone in the room was breathing with a phlegmy rattle and someone else was snoring. A voice mumbled, " 'lizabeth, you stop it now . . . don't you do that, 'lizabeth . . . don't hurt that kitten or Mama will whup us . . ." From the barroom beyond the curtain came a shout and a crash, and then a muffled burst of laughter, which faded away as if the warm, heavy darkness had sucked it up.

I sensed the return of the man with the soft fingers before he spoke or touched me; it was as though my skin had become sensitive to his emanations. For a moment he hovered over me silently; then I felt the boneless touch of his hand on one of mine. His breath tickled my ear. "Here you are, punkin. On the table in front of you—can you see?" He guided my hand to the bowl of alcohol. "Sweet dreams, punkin." The sound of his steps as he moved away suggested he was wearing carpet slippers.

I curved my fingers around the bowl and drew it toward me, but hesitated before tasting it. Perhaps it was laced with chloral hydrate, the "knock-out drops" that figured so prominently in *Police Gazette* reports of life in the Tenderloin. But why would anyone waste chloral hydrate on the impecunious drunks who frequented Velvet Rooms, who were hard pressed to come up with the twenty-five-cent admission charge to oblivion?

No, there was a more realistic danger, I thought. My nose told me that the bowl on the table contained alcohol—but which kind of alcohol? Grain or wood— ethyl or methyl? I tasted the contents of the bowl with the tip of my tongue as I considered the question. If there were any economic advantage to serving wood alcohol, I was sure Crapaud's would not have hesitated. But since grain alcohol was as cheap or cheaper than wood alcohol, why would they bother? Especially since it could possibly cause the management damaging publicity among its Bowery clientele?

I took a swallow from the bowl. It ripped its way down my throat like a claw hammer. I gasped and held my breath until the pain went away and I could feel a pulsation of warmth spreading outward. Then I relaxed in my chair and gave a sigh.

Four hours, I thought. *Four hours until I can start for the Circus. Four hours to get my strength back. Four hours to sleep.*

I moved the bowl carefully to one side and put my head down

on my folded arms. I breathed slowly and deeply and began counting backwards from one thousand. But sleep would not come. Instead, the sounds in the room around me and beyond the velvet curtain seemed to grow louder and more insistent. I shifted my position, trying to find a softer spot for my head to lie, but it was useless. I had counted backwards to nine-hundred-and-thirty-two when I said "The hell with it" and took four more swallows from the bowl.

This time sleep came easily. In a minute or two I was insensible. I don't know how long I remained that way. The next thing I knew I was wide awake again, eyes wide and muscles tense, head pounding, neck and shoulder muscles aching, and my mind chilled in a flood of pure terror.

For a moment I didn't know what had awakened me. Then I heard the sound of a creature whimpering hopelessly in an extremity of despair. For a few moments the whimper continued, and then a voice burst out, "Not the teeth! Christ, they're so sharp! Get away, you bastard! Oh, God, get away!" There was a crash that might have been caused by a chair hitting the floor, and the sound of a body scrambling on the boards. The voice screamed, "Oh, no, please, God, the teeth! The teeth!"

I heard the movement of another body and saw the suggestion of its shape in the darkness. I heard the soft scuffling of carpet slippers. "Oh, you mustn't make noise, sweetness. Very naughty—disturbs everybody's nappy-by. We'll have to stop it." The whispering voice was full of amusement. "Just make you forget those bad old teeth. Like this." There was a sound I couldn't identify, and the man on the floor screamed again. But it was a different kind of scream. The first time it was full of terror; this time it was the cry of unendurable pain.

I heard myself call out, "Hey! What's going on?"

"Nothing to worry about, lambkins. Just a little case of the horrors. You go nighty-night, now." There were more movements, and the chair was set upright and the man on the floor was helped into it. "Now, don't make me come back," the whispering voice suggested. "Next time you might hurt yourself."

There was a wrenching series of sobs that faded into deep gasps for breath. The carpet slippers scuffled across the floor, and once again the sounds from the barroom were the loudest noises I could hear.

I put my head down on my arms again and began to count backwards. But before sleep could come, the memory of Marya Perlman entered my mind, and I found myself reliving the night we had spent in each other's arms. I remembered her tenderness and her brutal passion, her disciplined control that exploded into wanton indulgence. *Ah, Marya,* I thought, *will we ever be good comrades helping each other again?*

I shifted my head on my arms in search of a softer pillow. Remembering Marya brought the image of her uncle to my mind. How was it possible that Hochmuth was Marya's uncle? How could such a desiccated stick be related to a creature of fire and storm? And what about my future, working for Hochmuth at *The Spirit of the Times*? Unless Marya could be cleared of the charges against her, I *had* no future. I was certain of that. But even if I survived this interminable night and found the evidence I sought, could I then count on Hochmuth's gratitude and support? *Ha,* I thought to myself bitterly. For the fact was that nothing on earth could ever make Hochmuth grateful and supportive of me.

I wondered what time it was. Judging from the noise beyond the curtain, it was the shank of the evening, eleven or twelve, perhaps as late as one. I had another two hours to wait.

I took four more swallows from my bowl, shuddered, and addressed myself to sleep.

I woke with a start and, for a moment, could not identify the cause of my awakening. The noise from the barroom had diminished to a gentle hum, and the nocturnal sounds around me were quiet and regular. I opened my eyes and raised my head from my arms.

A man took shape in the darkness. He was standing over me,

leaning forward, and I could feel one of his hands moving in my right trousers pocket. Instinctively I grabbed his wrist. "Oh, no you don't!" I said.

He straightened, making no effort to withdraw his hand from my grasp. "Hello, punkin. Go back to sleep now, that's a good little lush." He put his other hand on the back of my neck, and I felt the tips of his thumb and one finger press into the hollows under my ears. Deliberately he advanced the other hand in my pocket.

Bright rage flashed flaming pinwheels before my eyes. Thrusting upwards from my chair, I brought my free hand around into his belly with all my strength. He grunted and increased the pressure on my neck. A jagged bolt of pain exploded in my brain, and my forehead rapped the table top.

"Now just stay like that," the soft voice murmured. His hand dug deeper and encountered the few coins at the bottom of my pocket. "This all there is? What a shame. You've disappointed me." His fingers closed on the coins, and he began to withdraw them. I let go of his wrist, then seized a handful of the soft flesh that hung over his belt and twisted savagely. It hurt him; he growled and pressed my face hard against the table top. I clutched at the hand on the back of my neck and managed to get a grip on one thick finger, which I begun to bend back. He pulled his other hand out of my pocket and struck me across the cheekbone. I rolled my head to one side and suddenly felt free of his other hand. I threw myself out of my chair and landed on my knees on the floor.

I could see clearly enough in the darkness to make out his features. He had a wide, short, snoutlike nose and a mouth that hung open in a witless grin. He stood motionless, flexing the fingers of both hands. "Oh, my," he whispered, "what I'm going to have to do to you now!" He took a gliding step toward me.

I rose to my feet and met him standing up. We grappled, and each tried to knee the other without success. His arms wrapped around my chest, and he began to squeeze. I struck at his eyes with one hand and punched him behind the ear with the other. He lowered his head and buried his face in my shoulder. I felt his teeth closing on flesh. His bear hug tightened; I couldn't breathe; the blows I rained on the back and sides of his head were as harmless as a baby's pat-a-cake. I heard my spine and ribs creak, and then the sound was blotted out by a roaring in my ears. *It's the end of the road, Moretti,* I thought. *And what a place you picked to die!*

I had begun to slide into unconsciousness when I felt the bear hug ease. I opened my eyes. The face of my antagonist was in front of me, twisted upward toward the ceiling. Around his thick neck was an arm no wider than a yardstick, and over his shoulder, I saw the thin, wild face of a mad monk in an El Greco painting.

The man hung on him with one arm and hammered blows on his head with a stoneware alcohol bowl. His voice was a trembling thread of sound. I couldn't understand a word he said, but I recognized the voice; it belonged to the man who had called out in fear of the teeth earlier during the night.

My antagonist was surprised by the attack, but not hurt. I realized that he would rid himself of the gadfly on his back in a moment. If I were to take advantage of the interruption, I had to do it immediately. I stepped back and kicked the brute in the groin. My accuracy was perfect. He gave a gasp, bent his knees, and began to jackknife. The creature on his back gibbered in glee and continued to rain blows on his head. I hit him on the side of the jaw with a looping haymaker as he was going down. His knees struck the floor. He put his arms out in front of him to break his fall. I kicked him in the head and his arms turned to rubber. He lay gasping on the floor with the El Greco monk on his back, still pounding his skull with his alcohol bowl.

I touched the thin little man on the shoulder. "This isn't the D.T.'s any more, friend," I whispered. "We better get out of here fast."

He looked at me without comprehension. His eyes were perfectly round. He said "Hee! Hee! The teeth! Bite 'em! Swallow, chew, eat 'em!" He continued to strike the head in front of him. I reached to take the bowl from his hand, but he shied away and raised it threateningly at me.

"All right," I said, raising my hands in a placating gesture. "Keep up the good work. Pardon me if I leave now."

I found my way to the pencil line of light that marked the bottom of the curtain, drew it to one side, and stepped into the barroom. No one tried to stop me as I walked out onto the street.

10

Center Ring
at the Circus

A CHURCH CLOCK was chiming three o'clock when I turned the corner of Eighth Avenue and Eighteenth Street.

Eighteenth Street was utterly deserted. I felt as if I were entering the City of the Dead. I tried to walk lightly, but the sound of my steps echoed in my ears like the pounding of a fist on the door of an empty house. I kept to the shadows and tried to avoid the occasional light spills from the street lamps, although it seemed impossible any living eye would see me cross them.

I approached the Circus on the far side of the street. No glint of light escaped its curtained windows. I stood in the shadows for two or three minutes, watching and listening for any sign of life. When none was forthcoming, I crossed the street quickly and entered the shadowed areaway that ran beside the building.

I held my breath as I approached the side door. I touched the doorknob tentatively, lest it rattle. When it didn't, I grasped it firmly and, breathing a prayer, tried to turn it.

It wouldn't turn.

I tried to turn it the other way, with equal lack of success. I pressed it inwards, pulled it outwards, tried to raise it and lower it as I twisted. The knob was immovable.

A wave of futility swept over me and I almost groaned aloud. *Of course the door's locked,* I thought bitterly. *Why wouldn't it be? Maybe Bunny didn't get the message to her sister—maybe Maisie doesn't work there anymore. Maybe she's sick. Or maybe she just wants to keep her nose clean. And who could blame her?*

I leaned against the wall beside the locked door and passed my hand over my face. The absurd tenuousness of my plans was suddenly revealed to me. What was I doing here? I had come to search for evidence of the ownership of the Circus, in hopes that such evidence might suggest a motive for the murder of Tim Kanady that would divert suspicion from Marya Perlman. But how did I know that such evidence existed? And if it did, how did I know that it could help Marya? Logic told me I was following the most unpromising of strategies, as well as one of the most dangerous. How had I ever convinced myself I had a chance of success?

I shook my head to clear it of foolishness and free it for a realistic appraisal of my present situation. The first thing to do, obviously, was to get myself safely away from this dark and dangerous building . . .

The lock on the door gave a loud click. It was the sound of a dead bolt being turned back.

For a moment my heart stopped. I stood rigid, poised for flight toward the street if the door should open. But as the long moments succeeded one another, it became apparent the door was not going to open. The silence continued unbroken.

It's Maisie—she's unlocked the door! The darling girl came after all!

My fears forgotten, I stepped back to the door and twisted the knob. This time it turned easily in my hand. I heard the snick of the latch as it withdrew. I pressed gently and the door swung open without a sound.

Maisie Goertz stood inside, silhouetted against the soft light behind her. She was wearing an unbelted wrapper which she held closed with her crossed arms. Her dark hair hung loosely

153

to her shoulders. I stepped close to her and turned her body so I could see her face in the light. Her eyes were fringed black holes in her pale face, and her lips were bruised and swollen. She stared at me unblinkingly, and her body was rigid; she was paralyzed by fear. I touched her cheek with its clown's circle of rouge—it was cold. "Maisie, thank you," I whispered. "I was afraid you weren't coming."

She shook her head and pressed her fingers against my mouth. Her lips formed the word "No!" as she expelled her breath silently. Her expression was unbelieving, as if she couldn't accept the enormity of her transgression in admitting me to the building.

I put my face closer. "Is Klepp upstairs?" I breathed almost inaudibly.

She pulled away from me and shook her head again. Then, with a final despairing look, she turned away and hurried down the hall and through a door at the end. I was left standing alone between the outside entrance and the spiral staircase that led to the upper floors. I began to climb it gingerly, testing every tread before I put my full weight on it. When I reached the third floor, I raised my head like a soldier peeking over the top of a trench. The hallway leading to Axel Klepp's office was empty.

I took two quiet steps along the uncarpeted corridor and then froze as I heard a door open. It was on the left, and as it swung outward I grabbed the doorknob of the door nearest me and turned it. As I slipped through, I saw the broad-shouldered figure of Sharkey emerge into the hallway.

I closed my door, leaving only a slit to peek through. As I watched, Sharkey walked directly across the hall to a door on my right, which he opened with a key. He entered and closed the door behind him.

I opened my door and let in enough light to inspect my surroundings. I was in a small, unfurnished room with a bare floor and peeling wallpaper. Reassured that I had nothing to fear as long as I stayed where I was, I pulled the door to and applied my eye to the slit again.

For a minute or two the hall remained empty. From somewhere in the house, I could hear a piano playing—it was "Oft in the Stilly Night," I think, rendered with much sentiment—and there was a bray of masculine laughter and the tinkle of broken glass. The thought occurred to me that perhaps Sharkey had retired to his bedroom for the night. In that case I was wasting valuable time needlessly by cowering in an empty room. But would Sharkey be likely to keep his bedroom locked?

I decided to count to thirty, and if he didn't reappear by then, to leave my refuge and continue down the corridor. I was at twenty-two when his door opened again. He stepped out and then turned back to the room. "Don't worry—it won't be long now," he said in a sardonic voice. He closed the door and locked it, slipping the key into his waistcoat pocket.

"Hey, you there—yes you, my man," called a voice from just outside my door. I heard footsteps pass by, and then a man appeared in the slit between door and jamb. He was wearing a tuxedo, and the roll of fat on the back of his neck stood out like a ruff. He waved one hand imperiously. "The exhibition room— seem to have mixed my directions up. Show me the way, that's a good fellow."

Sharkey turned to look at the man, which meant that he was also looking almost directly at me. I gave a silent prayer that the aperture through which I was peering was narrow enough to escape his notice. An expression of rage passed across his face and was replaced almost instantly by an ingratiating smirk. "Why, certainly, sir. We wouldn't want you to miss anything. Right this way, sir." He crossed the hall and opened the door by which he had entered, and held it open as the man in the tuxedo stepped through. The door closed behind them, and once again the corridor was silent.

I opened the door and continued along the hall. I reached the white-painted door to Klepp's office without further incident. The knob turned smoothly under my hand, and I opened the door cautiously. The room was empty.

I pulled the door closed behind me and heard the latch click. *You're here at last, me lad,* I thought. *Now let's hope there's something for you to be here for.* I looked around the room, taking in details I hadn't noticed the first time. The red and black Chinese Chippendale desk was before me, as I had remembered it, but now I saw it was flanked by two black enameled filing cabinets, each the same height as the desk. A couch and an armchair were to one side of the desk, and a large combination bookcase to the other. On the walls was an odd collection of pictures —two misty Rhine castles, a copy of Rosa Bonheur's "Horse Fair," a Currier and Ives skating scene, and a very large Chinese painting on cloth showing a man standing on a bridge in front of a pagoda and looking with approval at a flowering cherry tree. Behind and a little to the left of the desk was a low wooden railing which formed a square about a yard across.

I walked carefully to the desk and circled it. It had four drawers in each pedestal and a wide drawer in the center. The flanking filing cabinets had two high drawers each. All the drawers in the filing cabinets and the center drawer of the desk were locked. I checked the contents of the other desk drawers and found them either empty or containing innocuous office supplies.

Before I attempted to break into the locked drawers, I thought I'd better inspect the office for other hiding places. I looked behind the two Rhine castles, the Bonheur copy, and the Currier and Ives and found only unbroken wall. But behind the Chinese wall hanging was a safe, very compact, very modern, and very firmly locked. It looked as if it would offer a formidable challenge to even the most accomplished yegg.

I let the wall hanging drop and turned to the low wooden railing which rose to a height of two feet from the floor. Why would anyone want to fence in a square yard of floor area, I wondered.

I looked down into the enclosure, expecting to see the same carpeting that covered much of the rest of the floor. Instead, what I saw was a heavy curtain placed in a horizontal rather than a vertical position. Along two opposite sides, the curtain was secured to rods by means of large wooden rings, and pull-cords ran to a brass cleat along the railing between the two rods.

I loosened the cords from the cleat and pulled them. Smoothly the curtain slid to the left along the rods, exposing a sheet of glass. Through the glass I could look down into the room below, but I doubted whether any of the people below could look up at me. Not if, as I was sure, it was a one-way mirror.

The room I looked into was divided into two halves; on one side, it was furnished like a gentleman's club, with dim lights, red leather chairs, and smoking stands to hold drinks and tobacco; on the other, it was a stage, a raised platform with curtains and footlights. The curtains were open and an exhibition was in progress. The action involved two women, one of whom was Maisie Goertz.

I stared down on the perverse spectacle with fascinated horror. In the darkened half of the room, cigars glowed and shadowy figures shifted in their chairs, crossed their legs, drank their drinks. In front of the lights the two women strained, twisted, arching their bodies, grinding their hips. Maisie's eyes were closed and her painted mouth gaped in real or simulated abandon. Her small breasts rose and fell rapidly with her breathing and her bare skin gleamed with sweat. The other woman, a husky Negress, looked as slippery as a wet bar of soap.

Then two newcomers arrived on stage.

One was a man, naked except for the black hood over his head. His athletic body was absolutely hairless and shone in the footlights like a statue of Carrara marble. He was well endowed and ready for the work at hand.

The other was an Irish wolfhound almost as big as a Shetland pony.

As the two new players entered into the game, I almost gagged on the returning taste of grain alcohol. I became aware of the sound of my own breathing, harsh and unsteady, and only a burning itch in my eyeballs reminded me to blink. In intense self-disgust, I thought, *will you look at yourself, Moretti? No better than the greenest hayseed in the Men Only tent at the county fair!* I told myself I woud pull the curtain closed and get on with my search—if not this second, then certainly the next.

My self-discipline was not put to the test, for at that moment the doorknob turned and the hall door began to open.

I threw myself behind the desk and scrambled into the knee-hole as footsteps entered the office and voices continued an ongoing conversation. A voice I recognized as Axel Klepp's was saying "—matter of time, I should think. Unless he's left town, of course. But somehow I don't think he has—he's the kind of fellow who would rather stay and joust with windmills. So I think we'll find him. I certainly *hope* we find him, don't you, partner?"

Another voice grunted in the affirmative.

Klepp's voice continued, as he moved toward that part of the room containing the couch and armchair, "He fits into the picture so nicely, hiding the Perlman woman the way he did. And that newspaper yearbook—I just *love* that newspaper yearbook!" There was the sound of bodies settling on upholstered furniture. Klepp said, "It's all right, Sharkey. You may sit too."

"Thanks, Mr. Klepp," Sharkey said, and I heard him do so.

"He was seen on the Bowery tonight, you say," Klepp said thoughtfully. "What time was that?" Sharkey answered it was about nine-thirty. "And then he threw Low-Boy halfway across a saloon and hared off down the street, is that right?" Sharkey said it was. "Then where did he go?" Klepp asked himself. "Not to his apartment. Not to his office. Not to the Perlman woman's room. Is he holed up in some bar? He couldn't be outside somewhere, could he? Sitting on some park bench right out in the open?"

"The cops are looking for him as hard as we are," Sharkey answered. "If he was on a park bench, they'd have him by now."

"Then he's at a friend's place, or with a woman, or in a bar. What about his friends, and his women?"

"He ain't got no real close friends, as far as we can tell. And except for Perlman, most of his women were ten-minute specials."

Crouched under the desk with my knees crowding my chin and my right arm asleep, I felt a sudden poignant stab of loneliness. *It's the God's truth,* I thought. *It's a wretched, friendless, thankless life I lead, and one that's far from the eye of Grace. And if I get out of this pit of corruption alive and in one piece, I'll be a better man for the rest of my days, I swear it!*

"If he's in a bar, they'll shoo him out in the next few minutes, if they haven't already, and our people on the street should find him— or the police will, which is the next best thing. In either case, he'll stop being the minor problem he is now. I refuse to worry about it anymore." Klepp's voice lost its edge of concern. "How about some brandy, partner? I have a bottle of Grand Armagnac here that must be tasted to be believed."

Another voice said, "O.K."

I heard Klepp rise from the couch and walk toward the desk. His legs and feet appeared at the kneehole of the desk and disappeared on the other side. A moment later he said, "This is odd!"

Sharkey asked, "What's that, Mr. Klepp?"

"The curtain over the observation window. I would have sworn it was closed the last time I noticed it. Have you been indulging your voyeuristic tendencies, Sharkey?"

"Huh? Me? No, I ain't been in here tonight, Mr. Klepp."

"No? Well, someone has." His legs reappeared in the kneehole. "And unless I'm very much mistaken, someone has also been looking through my desk— one of the drawers is sticking out a half-inch, which is not the way I leave them." He pushed the telltale drawer closed and tested the locked drawers one by one. "These are all right," he announced. "If somebody was trying to find anything important, he didn't succeed, which means—" He hesitated, and then went on crisply, "Partner, we may have been burgled tonight, and the burglar may still be on the premises. I suggest we institute a search for him immediately." I heard the sound of the other two men rising. "Sharkey, you start on this floor and work down. Try not to frighten any of the customers too much. Partner, why don't you and I go downstairs, check out the wine cellar, and work our way up? I'll give you a bottle of the Mouton Rothschild to take home with you. All right?"

I heard the sound of their footsteps moving toward the door, the door opening, the door closing. Then silence. I waited. The silence continued. After fifteen seconds or so, I shifted to a new position so I could flex the fingers of the hand that had gone to sleep. I discovered I had a painful crick in my neck. I crawled out of the kneehole and raised my head above the desk top.

"Good evening, Mr. Moretti, or rather, good morning," said Axel Klepp pleasantly. He was standing alone just inside the door, casually elegant in a belted velvet smoking jacket and dress trousers, with a silk scarf knotted loosely around his neck and a gleaming silver-mounted revolver in his hand. He held the pistol negligently, but its barrel pointed unwaveringly at my head. I straightened my knees and rose to my full height, raising my hands until they were even with my shoulders. "Good morning right back at you," I said through dry lips.

"I thought you might be hunkering down here, so I stayed to see," he continued in his low, melodious voice. He smiled in comfortable self-congratulation. "Needless to say, I'm delighted."

"I came here looking for a story, Mr. Klepp. Maybe you wouldn't mind answering a few questions for me, so I could pass the information along to my editor, who of course knows exactly where I am and would report my disappearance to the police in case I didn't get back to him."

Klepp threw his head back and laughed with genuine delight. "Oh, Mr. Moretti, your editor doesn't know where you are. Neither do those two Italian thugs you had protecting you at Gravesend. I'm very much afraid *nobody* knows where you are, or cares. Present company excepted, of course." Without taking his eyes off me, he opened the hall door behind him and called, "Sharkey! Partner! Come back a minute, will you?"

He moved to one side as two men entered the room. The first was Sharkey, whose vicious eyes first widened in surprise and then narrowed in anger at sight of me.

The second was Harrison Cobb, imposing in beautifully cut tails, with small diamond studs winking from his snowy dress shirt. He stopped on the threshold as he saw me. "Moretti!" he said harshly. "So it's you!"

"Certainly it's he, partner," Klepp said condescendingly. "Who else would it have been? That's not the question I'm interested in. The question I'm interested in is who let him in?" He regarded me thoughtfully a moment. "I don't suppose you care to tell us, Moretti?"

I shook my head. "I don't suppose you care to believe I accidentally found the side door open?" I countered.

Sharkey took a step toward me. "Want me to beat it out of him, Mr. Klepp?" he asked eagerly.

Klepp shook his head. "Oh, I think not. There'll be time for that kind of thing later."

Harrison Cobb said, "He came here to go through your files, Klepp."

"But he didn't find anything, did he? And even if he did, what good is it going to do him now? I'm afraid that after tonight Mr. Moretti isn't going to be able to tell anybody anything. Mr. Moretti is about to become a casualty in the cosmic struggle between Virtue and Wickedness."

My eyes searched the room desperately for a way out. I lowered my hands casually and shifted my weight to my toes. "Since my interest in your affairs is about to become academic, would you mind telling me about Tim Kanady's murder? Purely to satisfy my own curiosity, you understand." I dropped my right shoulder slightly and rested my right hand on the desk top. "Why was the poor man blown to smithereens?"

Klepp shrugged. "A simple business disagreement, Moretti. As a partner, Kanady offered certain assets—primarily in the areas of political patronage and police protection. Unfortunately, he wanted a larger share of the profits than these assets were worth. Mr. Cobb was anxious to replace Kanady as a partner, and I felt such a change would be for the best."

"Why the bomb?" I asked. "Why not just let your friend Sharkey here cut his throat and drop him in the East River?"

Klepp smiled like a pedagogue who had been asked to discourse on his favorite subject. The revolver in his hand dipped slightly and now pointed a few degrees to my right. "An ordinary murder could have pointed to ordinary motives, such as cupidity," he explained. "But an assassination, particularly a bombing, pointed to a motive of a political nature. Bombs are used by anarchists. By a delightful coincidence, Kanady was threatened by an anarchist in Union Square in front of a thousand witnesses. It seemed too choice an opportunity to ignore."

Cobb had been listening to Klepp's explanation with growing irritation. Now he said, "For God's sake, you'll be showing him the Circus's books next! You do love the sound of your own voice, Klepp!"

"When I consider the alternatives, I do for a fact," Klepp agreed. He smiled at me. "You've been very bothersome, Moretti, do you know that? First by sniffing around the Circus for the motive for Kanady's murder—I hated the idea that anybody would suggest a connection between the two—and second by keeping Marya Perlman out of the hands of the police and thus delaying the final resolution of the comedy."

"Did you send the bomb to Kanady's office?" I asked.

His eyebrows shot up. "I? Certainly not! I'm an entrepreneur, not a dynamiter!" He turned to glance at Cobb. "Would you like to elucidate, partner?"

Cobb growled, "I'm getting a little tired of this. What are we going to do with him?"

"Why, neutralize him. Along with our other guest. But not for a few minutes yet. I want to be sure all the customers are gone first. There's no reason to take any chances now—the game is in our hands." He said to me with a slight frown, "But

Moretti, I still want to know how you got in here tonight. It's disquieting to think you might have a confederate in the Circus."

I sighed and let my shoulders slump in apparent dejection. "I'll make a deal with you, Mr. Klepp. You let me walk out of here in one piece tonight, and I'll not only forget everything I've heard here—I'll tell you how I got in besides."

Klepp looked at me curiously from under his drooping eyelids. "Why, that sounds fair enough. We're not malignant men, are we, partner? Live and let live, that's the rule we live by. Very well, you have our word." He didn't take the trouble to try to lie convincingly. "Who let you in, Moretti?" he asked, forming his mouth around my name as though it tasted bad.

"Well, on the understanding we have, and taking you at your word—" I stopped and, staring wide-eyed at Harrison Cobb, cried, "NO! DON'T!"

Klepp was caught unprepared. Before he could make a conscious decision to ignore this hoary ruse, his gaze flickered away from me and toward his partner. I threw all my weight on my right hand and arm, straightened my legs, and vaulted over the corner of the desk. I was in midair when Klepp fired at me. I felt the tug of the bullet as it passed through the fullness of my jacket at the waist.

My feet cleared the low wooden railing and I crashed down on my heels on the observation window. The glass exploded under me. I covered my face with my raised arms as I began my descent. I felt shards of broken glass ripping through my clothes. Voices shouted in the room behind me—and then I was through the floor and falling into the exhibition room.

I landed on the stage, just behind the footlights, with my knees bent and my head shielded. I immediately rolled forward and crashed on my back with all the wind knocked out of me. Around me women screamed, men cursed, and a dog barked furiously. I stared straight up at the ceiling and into the face of Axel Klepp, framed by jagged points of glass.

"Get him!" Klepp screamed. "Hold him there! Don't let him get away!"

I pulled my feet under me and started to rise. The naked black Amazon in front of me stared at me wildly and cried, "Lord, it's the devil come to carry me to hell! Get away from me, devil!" She swung her fist at my head and caught me a blow on the ear that knocked my eyes out of focus.

I struggled erect. The male performer in the black hood came at me, his hands extended. Behind him was Maisie Goertz, her face distorted with fear. As his slippery fingers clutched at my face, she threw herself against his back and wrapped one leg around his knees. He stumbled, and I helped him down with a blow to the back of his head. For a second Maisie's head and my own were close together. "Get out, for God's sake," she gasped.

I started to run for the door. To reach it I would have to jump from the stage and pass through the spectators, most of whom were now on their feet calling questions to one another. I crossed the footlights and leaped into midair.

The Irish wolfhound got me, as bird hunters say, on the rise.

I felt his teeth close on my ankle as I was sailing toward a man with a brandy balloon in one hand and a cigar in the other and an expression of disbelief on his multichinned face. I twisted in the air as I looked over my shoulder to see what had attached itself to me, and both the dog and I were off balance when we landed. I slammed into the man with my chest in his face and one knee in his belly. All three of us crashed into a chair which overturned and dumped us in a shouting, snarling, struggling mass on the floor.

My first problem was the dog. *You brute, would you eat a leg off me?* I thought as I kicked his snout with my other foot. *And they call you Irish!* He shook his head stubbornly and hung on, growling. I kicked him again. *Let go, damn you! I haven't got time for this!* The man under me began bellowing for help, his soft body quaking with every cry. I kicked the dog a third time and felt his grip on my ankle loosen. I jerked my leg back and heard the ripping of my trousers. I began scrambling on my hands and knees. I felt the fat man's face under one hand, the mouth wide open. I pushed on. Someone landed on my back, and hands clutched at my arms. I rolled to one side, twisted, and scrambled ahead. *If I can just get out that door—*

Then the wolfhound clamped down on my ankle again, and I collapsed on my face.

Above the babble of voices around me, a familiar voice said, "Gentlemen, please. If you'll just step back, gentlemen—we'll see you're not inconvenienced any more, gentlemen—if you'll just let us, through, please."

I raised my head to see Axel Klepp's face join the ring of faces above me. A moment later, Cobb's and Sharkey's appeared beside his. The dog tightened his grip on my leg and a spasm of pain shot up my body. "Call off your dog," I said.

"Well, we've got you, you common burglar," Klepp said with satisfaction. He still held the silver-mounted pistol in his hand, and he pointed it at my head. "This thug broke into my office, gentlemen," he explained. "We caught him in the act, and he tried to escape."

"Have you called the police?" asked a worried spectator.

Klepp smiled. "Everything will be taken care of, gentlemen, rest assured of that. Without any notoriety, without any disturbance of any kind, believe me. Please sit back down—the entertainment will begin again in a few moments." He lowered his voice. "You, there—get up on your feet. Sharkey, get that dog off him."

I rose slowly, then took a deep breath and announced, "These men intend to murder me. They haven't called the police at all. I'm not a burglar, I'm a re—"

Klepp's pistol dug into my side. "Do you want to die right here?" he hissed.

I stopped. A glance at the faces around me showed that Klepp's version of the situation was accepted without question. Nor did I think that the whoremaster would hesitate to shoot me if I tried to continue my explanation. I bit my lip and lowered my eyes.

"All right, burglar— out," Klepp said, pushing me toward the door with the barrel of his pistol. The crowd opened to let me through, and I walked out of the room with Klepp and Cobb behind me. As we left I heard Klepp say, "Stay here and get things started again, then come upstairs," and Sharkey reply, "Yes, Mr. Klepp."

We went upstairs by the front staircase, which was wide and curved and deeply carpeted. The painting in the stairwell was startlingly erotic, but after the exhibition, it seemed as innocuous as Gainsborough's "Blue Boy." We walked along a hall past partly opened doors through which I could see women watching. I heard the sound of rustling garments, but no voices. At the end of the hall was a door and beyond it was the back hall that led to Klepp's office. But we didn't re-enter the office. "Stop right here, Moretti," Klepp ordered.

"What happens now?" asked Harrison Cobb in a worried tone.

"We put our friend on ice until our guests are gone." Klepp walked past me to the door that I had seen Sharkey open a half-hour before. He withdrew a key from his pocket and fitted it into the lock, still carefully keeping me covered with his pistol. "Cobb, would you mind getting a sheet out of the linen closet? It's the door on your right."

Cobb brought a sheet and, at Klepp's direction, tore it into six-inch strips. "Fine—now fold the strips over twice and tie his hands and feet together with them. They'll be as strong as ropes," Klepp said. Cobb began to bind my hand behind my back.

"I'm not entirely sure you've thought this out carefully," I said. "You just can't go along disposing of people whenever the thought strikes you—not when the people are connected by a logical chain. It's my sincere belief that killing me will turn out to be a source of deep regret to you before you're finished."

Cobb passed half a dozen turns of cloth around my wrists and tied a very tight knot, then another, then a third. Klepp said, "But you're forgetting—I told you *I* didn't kill the people you're referring to. When you asked me about Kanady, remember? I suggested it would be more appropriate for my partner to elucidate."

Cobb was wrapping a strip of sheet around my ankles. "You do love to run off at the mouth," he growled.

"So Cobb sent the bomb to Tammany Hall?" I asked.

"Part of the price of his partnership," Klepp said.

"And Eddie Terhune? Did Cobb blow him up too?"

"I've had just about enough of this" Cobb interrupted. He jerked the strip around my ankles, pulling my feet out from under me so that I fell heavily to the floor. He whipped a fresh strip around my face to cover my mouth. "See how much you can talk now!" he said viciously.

Klepp chuckled indulgently. "Well, bundle him up, partner. Tie him tight and stick him in. I don't know about you, but I could use a brandy."

Cobb secured the gag in my mouth as Klepp turned the key in the lock and opened the door. He stepped to one side. "In you go, Moretti," he said, as Cobb seized me by my coat collar and dragged me across the floor. He threw me over the threshold into darkness, and a moment later the door slammed behind me.

I could feel bare boards under my cheek. I lay perfectly still, listening to the footsteps that moved down the hall and into Klepp's office. In the silence that followed, I tested the knots at my wrists and ankles, rocking back and forth and straining my muscles futilely. Cobb had done an excellent job. I relaxed my arms and legs and concentrated on the gag over my mouth, opening and closing my jaws and pressing my tongue against the cloth. This seemed to offer some prospect of success. I kept at it and, after two or three minutes, was able to compress all the cloth within my mouth cavity, with space above and below for the passage of air. I tried an experimental shout, which emerged like the hoot of a drowning owl.

From close beside me, a low voice asked, "Who are you?"

With my tongue pinned against my lower teeth, I answered, " 'Addy Mmo'ettee."

"Who? And keep your voice down!"

" 'Addy Mmo'ettee! 'Addy Mmo'ettee!" I repeated. "The wepohtah!"

My fellow prisoner sighed in resignation. "Oh, hell," he said.

11

Plans for a Drive
by the River

CONVERSATION LANGUISHED until I loosened the gag sufficiently to push it out of my mouth entirely. Then I whispered,
"Warhull, is that you? What are you doing here?"

Sailor Warhull answered curtly, "Waiting for mommie to
come and tuck me in—what do you think? How tight they got
you tied?"

"Tight as a drum. My hands and feet are half asleep. How
about you?"

"Same with me. Been trying for hours and ain't gained an
inch. Bloody bastard knows his knots, and that's a fact."

"Well, we're neither of us gagged. Why don't we yell the house
down before all the customers go home?"

"Because the buggers would be on top of us before we get two
words out. Then we'd have the gags back in our mouths and
nothing to show for it."

"Anyway," I reflected, "Klepp told them I was a burglar and
he's holding me for the police. You're right—we're better off
keeping quiet."

We lay in silence for a few moments. I tried to think of hopeful outcomes to our predicament and came up with none. Then

Warhull whispered, "Roll over here next to me. I've got my back to you. You can work on my knots and I can work on yours."

It took a good deal of maneuvering in the blackness to reach a position where we were in touch with each other's bonds, and then we found our fingers were too numb to cope with the inflexible knots. I gave a groan. "It's no use, Warhull. Think of something else."

"There ain't nothing else," he said. "Keep flexing your fingers."

I relaxed my muscles and stared at the invisible ceiling above my head. "Tell me something, Sailor. Why are you in here?"

He hesitated before answering, and when he spoke, it was as if he had decided that the truth could hold no perils for him now. "Oh, the usual—I bit off more than I could chaw. Same's I've done before, just when everything's going smooth as cream. It's like some bloody voice inside me says, 'Get more! Get more!' and I can't do a damn thing except go ahead and grab."

"Bonnycastle?" I asked.

"Sure, Bonnycastle. He's a good horse, a fine horse. He would have run in the money in every race he was entered. Only that wasn't good enough."

"Was it your idea to run a ringer at the Elizabeth meet?"

He sighed. "No, it wasn't—not that I'm not as ready as the next man to make a bit of tin by driving up the odds—but it wasn't my idea at all. It was Terhune's."

"Terhune's?"

"Of course, Terhune's. Listen. Eddie Terhune liked the good life, but he wanted to get it on the cheap. He liked good food and good liquor, but it was better if he got it at a friend's house. He liked to sleep with beautiful women, but it was better if they were married to other men who paid their bills. So when he decided he wanted to start buying racehorses, he figured to get them at bargain prices from their owners."

"And he decided to start with Bonnycastle. Why?"

"Because he knew who I was. He knew my real name was

Warhull, not Wallens. See, Moretti, there's something you don't know about me—"

"That you were part of a horse-doping ring at Monmouth and got yourself barred from every track in the country? I know that. It took me a while to remember, that's all."

"All right, then. Eddie Terhune came to see me out at the stables, just after Mr. Cobb had been down to Lexington and had bought Bonnycastle. He comes up to me while I'm alone, and says, 'Well, Sailor Warhull, as I live and breathe! Done any doping lately, Sailor?' I pretends I don't know what he's talking about, but it's no good, he's got me dead to rights. He says he'd hate to tell Mr. Cobb who I really am, seeing as how it would get me fired and blacklisted all over again."

"But fortunately there was an alternative," I said.

"Yeah. The alternative was that I would find a real plater who looked like Bonnycastle and run him in enough races to convince Mr. Cobb to sell him for anything Terhune offered. Then I'd switch him back, and Terhune would get the McCoy. He'd have himself a champion stakes runner for five hundred tops."

"Where was the real Bonnycastle while you were running the plater at Elizabeth?"

Warhull laughed shortly. "Right in the Stillwater Farm Stables, right under Mr. Cobb's nose. I gave him a black wash, said he was a horse I had picked up at an auction, and offered to pay twenty dollars a month to board him there. Of course I had to slip the boys a few bucks to keep it buttoned up."

"And Cobb never caught on?"

Warhull snorted. "Of course he caught on—why do you think he's got me in this damned broom closet, for God's sake?" He was silent a moment, and when he spoke again his voice was fatalistic. "The first day of the Gravesend meet, the plater ran his third race. The odds were 30 to 1, and he finished dead last."

"I remember," I said. "I had twenty dollars on him."

"The more fool you. Right after the race Terhune made his play. He must have been too eager, because he tipped his mitt somehow. Cobb smelled a rat. That day after the races, he wrote me a note and signed it 'Terhune,' and had one of the stable boys deliver it to me. It said the deal was all set, and he wanted to pay me a bonus. Said to meet him at the Circus late Saturday night. When I came, that was all the proof Cobb needed. I been here ever since. Say, what day is it? Is it still Monday?"

I told him it was probably about four or four-thirty Tuesday morning. "Closing time. Klepp will be shooing out the last customers about now. After that I imagine it'll be our turn. To follow in the footsteps of Kanady and Terhune, that is."

His voice was suddenly edged with fear. "What do you mean? What about Kanady and Terhune?"

"They were both murdered, didn't you know that?"

"Kanady—he was blowed up by that anarchist woman. I read it in the paper. But what do you mean about Terhune?"

I repeated what Klepp had told me earlier about Kanady. "Strictly a business proposition. Cobb bought himself Kanady's share, using a bomb the police would think came from Marya Perlman. Exit Kanady, enter Cobb, a crazy revolutionary goes up the rope, and everybody lives happily ever after."

"But you said *Terhune*!" Warhull persisted.

"Just about the time you were coming here to the Circus Saturday night, Eddie Terhune was unwrapping a book in his apartment. There was another bomb inside. The police are supposed to think I sent it, because I'm sweet on Marya Perlman."

"Then Cobb—Cobb must have done it," Warhull said. "When he found out about the Bonnycastle switch. My God! He killed a man just for trying to take a few dollars from him!"

"Mr. Cobb is a sportsman who wants to win," I said.

"Then you're right—he's going to croak the two of us as sure as Hell. Oh, Lord, oh, Lord! Moretti, roll over here and let's try on them knots again."

I rolled on to my right side and jackknifed across the floor toward him. We bumped together in the darkness, as we had before, and a moment later my fingers touched the knots on his wrist. This time I was excited to discover a tingle of sensitivity in my fingertips. It was as though they were heavily coated with soap or tallow, but beneath the coating, they were still sentient.

"Hey, I think I can feel a little!" I whispered.

"So can I!" he answered.

I concentrated on one strand of one of his knots, clenching it between my fingernails and tugging it back and forth. My fingernails threatened to pull away from the quick, and I eased off for a moment. I lay listening, but could hear no sound except the labored breathing of Sailor Warhull. "How are you coming?" I whispered.

"Slow," he answered. "Too damn slow."

I began working my nails into the knot again. After a minute or two, I fancied I felt a little give in it. I grasped the weakened strand and tugged with all my strength, biting my lips against the pain. The strand slipped an inch, and then another, and then was free.

"I've got one," I whispered jubilantly.

I found another knot and selected an accessible strand. But before I could begin to work on it, I heard the sound of footsteps in the hall outside. I froze and, behind my back, could sense Warhull's tenseness.

As best I could tell, two people were passing the broom closet door. One was walking firmly with a heavy tread. The other steps were irregular and tentative; they scuffled, dragged, and struck lightly against the floor. We lay listening as the steps proceeded down the hall to Klepp's office, and his door closed behind them.

"Who do you suppose that was?" Warhull hissed.

"I don't know—but we better hurry!" I began to work on his knots with renewed energy and felt him do the same on mine. A few minutes later, he loosened one and moved to a second. We worked in silence, our breath rasping in the darkness. I could feel sweat turning cold on my face. I pulled a second knot apart, and so did Warhull. I clawed at the third knot, which was the last.

One of my fingernails had pulled so far off the quick it flexed back and forth as I worked—the pain was nauseating. I felt the third knot begin to give. "It's coming!" I gasped. "In a second, now—"

Then the knot slid open and Warhull's hands were loose. With a muffled exclamation, he rolled over, shook off the strip of sheeting from his wrists, and finished untying my bonds. In a moment, we were both sitting up and attacking the knots on our ankles—and then we were free.

On hands and knees I moved to the door and tried the knob. It was locked, and the lock seemed very solid. "They locked the door," I whispered to Warhull. "What can we pry it open with?"

I heard him moving in the blackness, and the sound of objects striking softly against one another. "Bucket—brooms—mop—bowl—sheets—wait a minute, there are some tools here in a box!" he whispered excitedly. "Here's a screwdriver and a hammer and a file—"

"Hand me the screwdriver!" I pawed for his hand and he passed it to me. It was a sturdy, eight-inch tool with a smooth wood handle and a blade a half-inch wide. I located the crack between door and door frame and pressed the blade into it, at a point slightly below the knob. It penetrated an inch, and I began to lever it back and forth. The wood creaked.

I felt Warhull's presence by my side. "Can you get it?" he asked.

"I don't know." I pressed harder and the wood creaked again, more sharply. I withdrew the bit a half inch and pulled the handle toward me. Wood splintered on the door frame. I moved the blade an eighth of an inch deeper and levered it again, and again heard wood splintering. "I think this will do it," I murmured. "Keep your fingers crossed."

As I pulled the screwdriver toward me again, I heard footsteps in the hall and the sound of Klepp's door closing. I froze. The footsteps approached, and I could hear the muffled sound of voices. Warhull breathed "Goddamn!" into my ear. I freed the screwdriver carefully from the door frame. The footsteps stopped in front of the closet door. Klepp's voice said distinctly, "The time has come, the walrus said——" and I heard the sound of a key entering a lock.

Warhull clutched my arm. "When he opens it—go for 'em!" he whispered.

I murmured my assent. The door swung open. The light was blinding. Then, as solid shapes coalesced, I threw myself forward onto the nearest of them.

It was Sharkey, and he stumbled backward. I was holding the screwdriver like a knife, with my thumb along the shaft, and I drove it toward his belly. The blade struck his belt buckle and the thrust was deflected, scraping along one side of his body. His arms wrapped around me, pulling me to the floor on top of him. As I fell, I saw Warhull collide with Harrison Cobb; he was brandishing a claw hammer over his head, and Cobb was struggling to take it away from him. Axel Klepp stood a yard away beside Maisie Goertz. Her eyes were wide and her mouth hung open. She was wearing a wrapper of some shiny material. Klepp held one of her arms; his other hand was in his jacket pocket.

Sharkey's hands closed over the screwdriver, and I felt it being twisted from my grip. I tugged furiously and felt myself losing. I decided to release my hold and run for it. But before I could, Klepp's pistol pressed against the side of my head.

"Stop it now, or I'll blow your brains out right here," he said levelly. I ceased all motion, and Sharkey pushed me to one side and got to his feet. "You too, Warhull— drop that hammer and stand still!" Warhull complied with a curse, and Cobb stepped back from him, straightening his dress shirt bosom and adjusting the fit of his coat. "Get up, Moretti," Klepp continued. "Slowly. And keep your hands at your sides." I complied. "Now let's all go back to my office. We have a bit of work to finish there."

Warhull and I walked toward the white-painted door. Klepp followed us, clutching Maisie Goertz's arm with one hand and covering us with the pistol in the other. Cobb and Sharkey brought up the rear. When we were inside, Klepp closed the door and gestured toward the couch. "I think you two better sit to-gether, where I can watch both of you," he said. "I've had about all the trouble I want from you, Moretti."

Warhull and I sat down. Klepp pushed Maisie into an arm-chair and then perched himself on the edge of his garish lac-quered desk. Cobb and Sharkey remained standing. Klepp ges-tured to Maisie with his pistol. "This slut let you in tonight," he said flatly.

"That's a lie," I answered. "I've never seen her before in my life."

Maisie's expression was a mixture of hope and despair, with the despair predominating. Klepp shook his head impatiently. "Stop it. I saw her try to help you in the brawl downstairs. One of the other girls remembers her leaving the room a few minutes earlier, when she must have let you in."

"You're wrong, Klepp. You've got traitors here, but she's not one of them."

His nostrils flared and his lips tightened. "I don't intend to debate the issue. Listen to me. I offer you a deal. Accept it and she lives. Reject it and she dies. It's just that simple."

"I tell you I never saw the girl before. Why should I give a damn about what happens to her?" I insisted.

"I don't know why you should. I don't know why she decided to help you, but she did. Whatever the reason, it's a fact—I accept it as a fact. Very well. This is the deal: You write me a short note and sign your name to it and she lives. Refuse and she dies."

Maisie's face was ashen. She watched me unblinkingly, and her body under the sleazy wrapper was perfectly still; it was as if she had forgotten how to breathe. I looked into her eyes. "And what would be in this note, if I should happen to write it?" I asked.

"It would express your remorse at having dynamited Eddie Terhune, which was due to your insane infatuation for Marya

Perlman, the anarchist. Nothing exhaustive—a line or two will suffice."

I shook my head incredulously. "It's a wonderful mess of nonsense you're talking, for a fact, Mr. Klepp. You're asking me to confess to a crime I didn't do to save a girl I've never met from a death she'll very likely receive whether I do it or not. Isn't that about the long and short of it?"

"Oh, for Christ's sake, Klepp —" Cobb growled.

The whoremaster raised his left hand. "Allow me. No, Moretti, it is not the long and short of it. In the first place, this is not a girl you've never met. This is a girl who was willing to run the risk of helping you invade my premises, for whatever reason, so I assume you have some slight feeling for her. Please don't argue. In the second place, you are wrong to conclude she'll arrive at the same end whether you ·ccede to my wishes or not. I tell you it is within your power to save her life. If you write the note for me, she'll live. If not, she won't. You, Moretti, will be her savior — or her executioner."

Maisie tore her eyes from my face and turned to Klepp. "Tell him the truth, why don't you, you toad? You'll kill us all, no matter what he does!"

Klepp gestured to Sharkey. Sharkey stepped across the thick rug as gracefully as an acrobat, poised in front of her on his toes, and struck her across the mouth with his open hand. The sound of the blow seemed as loud as a thunderclap. Her head snapped back against the chair and her eyelids squeezed closed. An angry flush spread across her face where his hand had struck. Warhull grunted and leaned forward on the couch, and I felt all my muscles tighten for action.

"Better not," said Klepp. The muzzle of his pistol moved between Warhull and me, waiting for one of us to declare himself the more immediate target. Warhull arrested his movement and I didn't begin mine.

Instead I said, "Don't hit her again. Tell him, Klepp. If you want anything from me, don't hit her again."

Klepp smiled. "That will do, Sharkey," he said. Sharkey straightened his jacket and stepped away from Maisie's chair, resuming his place against the wall. "Then I assume you're agreeable to my proposal?" he asked me.

"Wait a minute. In the unlikely, the *very* unlikely, event that I go along with this, what guarantee do I have that Mais—that this woman won't be hurt?"

"Oh, Moretti, women are a business to me, not a pleasure. I get no enjoyment out of treating them harshly, believe me. Not even when they betray my trust. This one"—he gestured toward Maisie as though she were a cow in a livestock sale—"has a number of good years left in her. Why should I waste them? Oh, I'm not saying I'll keep her here at the Circus, or even in New York City. Perhaps not even in the United States. Perhaps I might move her to Rio de Janeiro or to the Continent—"

"—or to a crib in Macao or a back alley in Djibouti," I interrupted.

He raised his shoulders an inch. "Consider the alternatives, as I always say. Is it better to be alive in Djibouti or dead in Chelsea?" He turned toward Maisie. "What do you think, my dear? Do you want to die tonight?"

"Can't you get on with it?" Cobb asked. His eyes were worried, and he rubbed his chin nervously with well-manicured fingers. "It's late as hell. The sun'll be up in an hour."

"I know," Klepp said. "What about it, Moretti? Will you write me my note?"

"There's a few more things to discuss before that," I said.

"No, you're wrong. There's nothing more to discuss," Klepp snapped. "In five minutes either all three of you go out that door, or just you and Warhull do. It really doesn't make that much difference to me whether the girl goes or not—it's up to you. But in five minutes you go. There's no more time for stalling, Moretti."

I swallowed. Klepp, Cobb, and Sharkey stared at me, waiting.

Maisie's eyes, red-rimmed and shimmering with moisture, gazed at me from shadowed sockets. Beside me, Warhull muttered a curse and shifted on the cushion.

"All right—hand me the pen and paper," I sighed.

"Come here to the desk and write what I tell you," Klepp ordered. I moved to the upholstered swivel chair and picked up a pen. Klepp put a sheet of note paper in front of me and I dipped my pen in the inkwell. "Begin it 'To whom it may concern,' and then say 'I confess that I planned and carried out the murder of Edward Terhune as a terroristic act against Tammany Hall, to continue the work begun by my lover Marya Perlman.'" Klepp stopped and pulled on his nose thoughtfully. I wrote the words as he directed. When I stopped, he continued, "'God damn the capitalistic system and the United States of America.' And sign your name, nice and legible."

I finished the body of the note, but placed my pen on the desk without signing it. "And after I put my John Hancock on it, what happens then?"

"The same thing that happens if you *don't* put your John Hancock on it—but it doesn't happen to your *petite amie* here. I've explained that to you."

"And would you like to tell me exactly what that will be?"

Klepp pushed his pistol into my face. I closed my eyes and jerked my head back just in time to prevent the muzzle from touching my eyeball. "Sign that note this instant, or I'll kill you where you sit," he said harshly. "I've just run out of patience."

I picked up the pen. "Sorry, Sailor," I said to my companion in disaster. "We made a good try for it." I wrote my name on the note paper. The writing was a bit unsteady and at one point the nib caught and sprinkled the surface with tiny ink spots, but the signature was legible enough. I blew on it and handed the note to Klepp, who inspected it and then folded it and tucked it in his pocket He turned to Sharkey and said, "Take the girl downstairs and have Dolan or Hardesty lock her up in the empty storeroom and make sure she doesn't get away. Then bring the carriage around to the front."

Sharkey moved toward Maisie, who rose without being told. She waited docilely as he took her arm and propelled her toward the door. Her eyes remained on my face. She did not speak, nor did I. The door closed behind them.

"Surprised that I'm keeping my word, Moretti? Oh, I often do, particularly when it's to my financial interest. Now let's wait for Sharkey to get back." Keeping Warhull and me covered with one hand, he unlocked a drawer in his desk and withdrew another revolver, this one without silver mounting. He handed it to Cobb. "You better take this along, partner, in case our friends get any more of their bumptious ideas."

Cobb frowned at the pistol. "Is this really necessary, Klepp? I've never gotten into the habit of carrying firearms."

"They're ugly and vulgar, there's no getting around that," Klepp said gravely, his eyes glinting with malice. "But sometimes, in the new business world which you have now entered, and in which you were so anxious to assume a partnership, it is not always possible to do your murdering at long distance, with bombs and other sanitary devices. Sometimes, partner, it's even necessary to get some blood on your hands."

"All right, I get your point," Cobb said sulkily. He slipped the pistol into his inside breast pocket. It ruined the fit of his tailcoat.

We waited in silence for Sharkey. He was back in five minutes. I noticed that he was wearing brass knuckles over his right fist. I wondered how many extra sets he kept on hand. "All set, Mr. Klepp," he said.

"Then let's be on our way. Sharkey, you go first. Moretti and Warhull, you keep three paces behind Sharkey. Cobb, you and I stay three paces behind them. *Allons, mes enfants!*"

We left the office and walked along the uncarpeted corridor

to the narrow circular staircase. Sharkey started down it, watching us over his shoulder as he descended. Warhull followed him, and I came third. Over my shoulder I could see Klepp and Cobb, Klepp with his pistol in his hand and Cobb with one hand under his coat lapel. We passed the second landing and continued downward. The house was as still as a tomb.

My mind was racing desperately. At the foot of the stairs, I stopped and turned to face Klepp. "Where are you taking us?" I asked through dry lips.

He paused on the steps. The muzzle of his pistol was an unwinking eye studying my face. "I thought we'd take a drive down by the river—it's lovely there, with the breeze, and the gulls feeding on the garbage."

"I won't go. Why should I make it easy for you? If you want to kill me, do it here!"

Klepp sighed. "You forget so soon. The girl, Moretti! She's stored away in the back, remember? Unless you come along quietly, I'm afraid I'll have to tell Sharkey to beat her to death with those brass knuckles he uses so skillfully. What a waste that would be, since it wouldn't change what happens to you one iota."

My shoulders slumped. I turned and walked along the short length of hall to the heavy oak door which Sharkey held open. He preceded Warhull into the areaway, walking backwards. The door began to swing closed and Klepp stopped it with one hand, holding it open for me and for himself. Cobb followed, and the door closed firmly behind us.

The night air was surprisingly cool and fresh. I took a deep breath and filled my lungs until they hurt. Overhead the stars were hidden behind a screen of cloud, and the moon only showed as a luminous patch in the sky. *It's as good a night for it as any other,* I thought, *but it's a long way from here to the river.*

Sharkey backed toward the street, moving slowly, his weight poised lightly on his toes. Warhull followed, his body swaying from one side to the other with his bowlegged sailor's stride. I moved after them. I could feel the proximity of the two men behind me.

We reached the street. There was a black coach standing at the curb, with a handsome gray horse between the shafts. Sharkey backed across the sidewalk and opened the door. Klepp touched me between the shoulders with his pistol and said, "Inside, please."

"Wait a minute," I pleaded, half-turning to face him. "I don't care about myself, but what about Marya Perlman? She'll be tried and convicted of a crime she didn't commit—a crime your partner planned and carried out for profit! Can't you do anything for her?"

Klepp chuckled in genuine amusement. "What an illogical man you are! That's the whole idea, don't you see? Why, if the police suspected she was innocent, they might start looking for someone who was guilty! Now, if you'll get into the coach—"

"MORETTI—GET DOWN!" cried a voice from my left, and as I turned in that direction, something sailed through the air toward me. I threw myself forward, colliding with Warhull and knocking him off balance. We both struck the sidewalk just as the night burst into flame.

12

Love as a
Revolutionary Act

THE CONCUSSION scooped up my body and flung it against
one wheel of the coach. I landed in a jackknifed position, upside
down, with my back and shoulders on the pavement and my
knees in my face, and a roaring like Niagara in my ears. I slid
down until I was horizontal, flat on my back in the gutter. Objects pattered down upon me.

The first thing I realized was that the coach was moving, the
panicky horse was tugging at the shafts, and the wheel that rose
above me was turning as it approached my outstretched arm. I
rolled free as the wheels rumbled past and raised myself on one
elbow until I could see over the curbing.

What had been two people lay on the sidewalk. The head and
upper torso of Alex Klepp lay near the entrance to the areaway;
one of his legs, with the foot still neatly shod, was fifteen feet
away in the direction of Eighth Avenue; the other, barefooted,
lay a few feet in the opposite direction. Most of Harrison Cobb
was sprawled near his partner. His handsome evening clothes
were shredded and almost all his head was gone.

Against the wall of the next building leaned Felix Algauer,
his small, broad-shouldered body slumped weakly and his head

buried in his hands. He was making gagging noises.

The fumes from the bomb rasped in my throat and nasal passages, and I began to cough. Tears blurred my eyes. I heard the clatter of the coach behind its runaway horse, now halfway down the block toward Ninth Avenue. I struggled to my knees, surprised that all my limbs seemed to be in working order. Behind me I heard Warhull's voice: "Oh, Christ! Oh, sweet suffering Jesus Christ!" I turned and saw him sprawled across the body of Sharkey in the street. Apparently the wheels of the coach had passed over Sharkey's face; what remained was hardly recognizable. His arms were spread out, his brass knuckles still on his right hand. Warhull struggled back from the body and got to his feet. His voice shook as he said, "He's dead, Moretti!"

"They're all dead," I said, gesturing toward the shambles on the sidewalk.

Lights were glowing behind windows on the other side of Eighteenth Street, although none showed from the curtained windows of the Circus. The tweet of police whistles sounded from three directions, and I could hear the clanging of a police wagon in the distance. I started toward Felix Algauer.

"The coppers!" cried Warhull. "Let's get out of here!"

"You lubber, this is the first time you've ever been on the side of the angels in your life!" I called over my shoulder. "Would you want to miss out on it now?"

*

Problems with the police went on for the better part of three days. First they wanted to charge Sasha with murdering Klepp and Cobb, and me with complicity in their murders as well as being solely responsible for the taking-off of Eddie Terhune. Then as things began to clarify, they modified their charges against Sasha to wanton endangerment, and against me to complicity in same. Finally they dropped all charges against me, although they were unwilling to do the same for Algauer, who was, they insisted, a practicing professional bomb-thrower.

Warhull was released before I was. So was Marya Perlman. I didn't have the opportunity to see her at the jail.

Hochmuth was no help in my hour of need. At first he told the police that my name was unfamiliar to him, and he would have to check his records. When forced to amend that statement, he declared that I was an incompetent malcontent chronically on the verge of discharge, whose assertion that the sun will rise to-morrow would need the support of an independent witness.

I presented myself at his desk on my first morning back at the newspaper office. He looked up at me from under his green eyeshade, his pursed mouth a horizontal dimple in his putty-colored face. "Moretti," he said expressionlessly. "We have been learning to get along without you for the past few days."

"Ah, I've missed you too, Mr. Hochmuth. But all's well that ends well, as the Bard says. And you must admit it's all ended well—for the young lady we were both concerned about, at any rate."

"Yes, I have read that a certain female of violent convictions and an ungrateful nature is now free to walk the streets again. I'm sure you are entitled to a fair share of the praise or blame for that, whichever may be your due. Also, I read that you were involved in the, ah, dismantling of Mr. Harrison Cobb, the good friend of The Owner, to whose suburban stables I despatched you some weeks ago. It is still to be seen how grateful The Owner will be to you for that."

"Mr. Hochmuth, you must know that Cobb was a double murderer as well as a pander, and it's the warmest kind of thanks I deserve from Mr. Monk for eliminating the spalpeen from his guest list!"

"We shall see, Moretti. We shall see. In the meantime, you will please prepare a brief report on the horse racing aspects of this lamentable business? I believe there was something in the *World* about a horse called Bonnycastle who was actually an entirely different animal?"

"Yes, sir."

"Very well. Restrict yourself to that. No bombs or bordellos. Two hundred words should suffice. Turn it in before you leave for Gravesend, please." He picked up a meticulously sharpened pencil and bent over a sheet of copy paper.

"Mr. Hochmuth," I said earnestly, leaning toward him across his neat desk, "I know you're not the man to take up office time for it, but I'll be glad to give you all the details about how I saved your niece from a terrible miscarriage of justice, if you'll join me for a sandwich this noon in City Hall Square, on the third bench from Broadway, facing south."

"Thank you, but that will not be necessary," he said firmly. "I have very little taste for sensationalism, and I'm afraid my lunch hour is already committed. To my pigeons. Good day."

During the afternoon at the track, I found my thoughts turning to Marya Perlman with disturbing frequency. After the races, I refused the offer of an evening of roistering with Clem Harber, pleading a previous engagement. I went directly to the *Police Gazette* building, where I sold Richard K. Fox a three-thousand-word story, dealing primarily with bombs and bordellos and only incidentally with horse racing, for sixty dollars. The pen name we selected was A Watcher from the Shadows, which I rather liked.

From the corner of Dover and Pearl streets, I walked north along the Bowery to Fifth Street. I turned right at the corner and entered the door under the sign that read Zum Groben Michel. As the door closed behind me, the clamor of disputatious voices sank to a murmur. No one looked directly at me, but every eye in the room was angled in my direction. The smell was still an amalgam of sweat, beer, cabbage, chicken fat, cheap tobacco, mouldering plaster, and sewer gas. The bartender moved his close-to-three-hundred-pounds toward me, his bald head, bisected by its purple scar, gleaming dully in the gaslight, "You want something?" he demanded.

"You remember me," I said. "I'll have a stein of your best. And tell me—would Marya Perlman happen to be here tonight?"

He glowered in silence as he filled my glass, set it in front of me, and pocketed my nickel. Then he leaned close and rumbled, "I am watching you."

His breath was like the blast from a furnace stoked with onions. I leaned away and picked up my stein. "I'll try to keep you entertained," I said.

I found Marya at a table near the back, beyond the dog-eared poster of the clenched fist with the broken fetter and the words "PROPERTY IS THEFT." She was sitting with a heavily bearded man in a suit two sizes too small for him. Their heads were close together as they bent over a sheaf of papers. I stepped up to the table and said, "Hello, comrade."

Marya glanced up and her eyes widened. She straightened in her chair and drew a deep breath. "Moretti—hello," she answered.

The bearded man looked up angrily. I saw that his beard covered an ugly pit in his jaw, a deformation as large as a baseball. "You see we are busy, comrade," he said in a harsh voice. "You are excused."

"He is not a comrade, Johann," Marya said. "He is Moretti, the reporter. He was there when Sasha threw the bomb."

"Ach, *der Berichterstatter!*" He smiled, although his eyes remained hostile. "Sit down, Mr. Moretti. We will make plans for you to attend the rally and bear witness."

I remained standing. "The rally?"

"The rally for Sasha, to demand his immediate release," Marya answered. "Johann and I are planning the publicity now."

"I'm not here to plan a rally, Marya. I'm here for a bit of private conversation."

She looked at me a moment in silence. Her indigo eyes seemed black in the artificial light. She brushed her short-cropped hair away from one small ear. Her lips turned up in the slightest of half-smiles, and she said to her companion, "Please give us five minutes, Johann. Go have a drink at the bar, *hein?*"

He glowered at me as he pushed his chair back and rose. I

187

took his place as he walked toward the front of the barroom. "How's your psychic energy, machushla?" I asked as I put my hand on hers.

She looked at me levelly. "There is something I have wondered. How did the police know that I was in your room?"

"I guess we'll never know for sure, but the first time I met Klepp at the Circus, I made the mistake of mentioning I had someone waiting for me at home. He must have put two and two together and tipped off the police. *Mea culpa, mea maxima culpa.*" I squeezed her hand. "Let's not be wasting our time rehashing these prosaic details. Come to Bleeker Street and let me smother you with salami sandwiches."

She shook her head. "Sasha is still in prison, still held by the enemies of the working class. The first order of business is to organize protests immediately." She withdrew her hand from under mine. "Johann is right, Moretti. You can appear at the rally and bear witness to the connivance of politicians and criminals that makes capitalism a stench in the nostrils of all mankind!"

I leaned toward her. "Comrades help each other," I said huskily. "Let's not be talking about all mankind. Let's be talking about the two of us. Come back to Bleeker Street with me."

Her bosom rose and fell. She closed her eyes and then opened them again. "Be serious, Moretti. There are things that must be done. The class enemies do not waste their time—neither must we! Won't you agree to be on the program?"

"Marya, listen to me. I care about you. Those days we were together—I've been thinking about them. I want some more, maybe a lot more. I want to go to sleep beside you very late and wake up beside you very early."

"Moretti—"

"We can explore New York together this summer. You can go to all the tracks with me—to Sheepshead Bay and Morris Park and Brighton and Saratoga. We'll go to Coney Island on Sundays! I'll buy you lobsters at Delmonico's! We'll have picnics in Central Park! We'll sit in a box at Tony Pastor's!"

"Moretti—" Marya said again. She set her square jaw and shook her head in frustration. "*Mashuggah!* Listen, we are not the same, Moretti. Yes, we went to bed together, we enjoyed each other, but we are not the same!"

"Sure, and wouldn't it be a sorry thing if we were?"

"You don't understand." She looked at me with sad determination, like a mother about to explain about Santa Claus. "I will not sleep with you tonight. I will sleep with Johann Most. Last week I slept with Sasha, on those nights when I wasn't sleeping with his cousin Fedya instead. When I slept with you, it was because I wanted to. That is the way it will always be with me." She paused, and her big dark eyes gazed into mine unblinkingly. "If we were living together and I went to bed with another man, how would you feel?"

"It wouldn't happen—but if it did, it would be because I wasn't doing what I was supposed to be doing. Why, if I were taking care of you the way I *would* be taking care of you, you wouldn't have room in your brain to think of any other man!"

"No, Moretti, it would be just the opposite. Just when you were filling my life most completely, that would be the time when I would *have* to think of another!" She leaned toward me and spoke with a vibrant intensity. "I must be free to love without obligation, without guilt, as a revolutionary act. If I felt bourgeois sentimentality begin to grow, I should cut it out like a surgeon cuts out a cancer!"

I made a pattern of wet rings on the table top with my beer stein. "I'm not sure we have the basis for a continuing relationship here," I said after a moment.

She smiled slightly. "I think perhaps you are right. I agree with your decision." She put her warm rough hand on mine briefly. "Now let us talk of important things. The protest rally for Sasha—will you come and speak?"

I glanced around the crowded, noisy room. The man she had called Johann was leaning against the bar and drinking a glass

of whiskey. He scowled at me as our eyes met. I raised one hand
in a beckoning gesture. "No, Marya, I don't think so," I said,
pushing back my chair. "I don't think I'd do too well fanning
the flames of class war. I don't think your Uncle Otto would
like it much, either."

"That *schmok*—"

"The very word. But unfortunately, he's still my editor."
Johann appeared beside the table, and I vacated the chair for
him. "Good-by, Marya," I said, bowing. "It's been an experience to remember. Good-by, Johann. Up the rebels!"

"Up the rebels," Marya said, raising her clenched fist.

I pushed my way between the crowded tables toward the street
door. I waved to the bartender. "I'm leaving—you can lower your
guard now!" I called. He glowered at me. I opened the door
and stepped out onto Fifth Street. It was a balmy evening, but I
shivered as though from a sudden chill.

*

A few days later I consulted a calendar and discovered it was
six weeks since the fateful day Liz Cochrane had inveigled me
into helping her invade McSorley's. I planned my evening ac-
cordingly, and a little after seven o'clock, I entered the hallowed
confines. The front room was crowded, Old John McSorley was
behind the bar, his bushy white eyebrows rising and falling like
acrobatic caterpillars as he argued with a customer about Home
Rule. I selected a clay pipe and stuffed it with the house shag,
lit it from the gas flame, selected a slice of crumbling cheddar
cheese from the free lunch, and joined them. "Good evening,
John," I said. "A stein of dark, if you please."

McSorley drew the glass and set it down before me. "Well,
Moretti—haven't seen much of you lately," he said genially.
"You getting too good for your old friends? Let's see, it must be
two, three weeks since you came by."

"You don't remember the last time I was here, John?"

"Not for certain. Why, should I? What did you do, get in a fight with O'Malley here?" He poked the customer beside me with a bony finger and chortled.

"I'd never do anything that crazy. John, give O'Malley a glass and have one yourself, and join me in a toast to this establishment of yours, which casts its welcome beam upon the drinking man like a lighthouse succors the storm-tossed mariner."

"Ah, I'll drink to that," cried Old John McSorley.

An hour later I felt a tap on my shoulder. I turned with an invitation to have a drink on my lips and found myself looking into the solemn eyes of Tomaso, whose topcoat was buttoned up to the neck in spite of the warm weather. His partner Gaetano was beside him, his head even with Tomaso's shoulder. "*Buona sera*, Patrizio," said Tomaso with formal courtesy, and Gaetano nodded to indicate the greeting covered him as well.

"*Buona sera*, gentlemen," I answered, and asked them to have a glass of beer with me. Tomaso shook his head and explained that they were on business and so must refuse. "Business?" I said, feeling a chill of apprehension. "You mean something to do with Klepp's people or the Circus?"

"Nothing like that, Patrizio. No, it is your promise to Don Paolo. Tonight is the party he told you of, for the eighteenth birthday of his wife's cousin's daughter Giuseppina, so that she may meet young men." It seemed to me he placed an ironical stress on the word *young*. "Don Paolo does not understand why you are not present, Patrizio."

I smote my forehead. "Then he wanted me after all? I thought it was only a formality, a gesture of courtesy to an unworthy member of the family! How could I know that *Zio* Paolo actually desired my attendance at such an illustrious event!"

Tomaso and Gaetano regarded me expressionlessly. I drained my glass and grabbed each of them by the elbow. "Well, let's go, let's go!" I cried. Tomaso bumped into a chair and I heard the clank of his *lupara* striking wood. "Mustn't waste a moment!

Make sure Don Paolo knows how anxious I am to arrive!" I tugged them through the crowded drinkers and out into the street.

Don Paolo's wife's cousin's daughter Giuseppina was much as I remembered her—skinny, sallow, and with a bite like a rabbit. She looked at me blankly when I introduced myself, obviously unable to place me at all. After two minutes of awkward pleasantries, I excused myself and headed toward the vino, bowing to Don Paolo en route. As I poured myself a glass, a soft voice said by my ear, "You don't remember me, do you, Patrizio?"

I looked up into warm brown eyes fringed with heavy lashes, tilted slightly in an oval face with a wide brow and a delicately rounded chin. Full red lips parted over perfect white teeth. The whole enchanting arrangement was framed by softly curling black hair. "Oh, yes—I— of course!" I stammered.

"I am your second cousin Rosamaria. No doubt you heard that I was widowed last year," she said, as the corners of her luscious mouth turned down in momentary sorrow.

—But this belongs to another story.

Author's Note

The Mafia made its first appearance in the United States in New Orleans in 1868–69 and shortly thereafter was established in New York City. Chief Inspector Byrnes recognized its existence in 1881, and by the middle of that decade, the Mafia (or Maffia, as it was often spelled) was a staple of sensational journalism. Tradition holds that the organization was formed in Sicily by Mazzini in 1860 on the orders of Garibaldi himself. One theory of the origin of the name is that *Mafia* stands for the initial letters of the words *M*azzini *A*utorizza *F*urti, *I*ndendi, *A*vvelenamenti (Mazzini Authorizes Thefts, Arsons, Poisonings). In a fit of pique after failing to get a conviction in a Mafia-connected East Side killing in 1889, Byrnes said, as far as he was concerned, Italians "could go ahead and kill each other." The result was the Mafia-Camorra War, lasting twenty-eight years, with 1400 murders and 2300 bombings.

The Black Hand, often mistakenly considered the forerunner of the Mafia, wasn't really an organization at all but an umbrella name assumed by free-lance extortionists and kidnappers. Many of the thugs who signed their terroristic notes with an inky handprint were not even Italian. The Mafia despised them.

Marya Perlman is of course modeled on Emma Goldman, and her friend Sasha was suggested by Goldman's lover and collaborator Alexander Berkman. A year or two after the period of this novel, Goldman and Berkman planned the assassination of Henry Clay Frick, the general manager of the Carnegie Steel Company, which was undergoing a lockout at the time. They had only enough money for one train ticket, so Berkman went to Worcester, Massachusetts, alone. He shot three bullets into Frick and stabbed him a number of times, but failed to kill him. He spent the next twenty years in prison.

Johann Most was a leading anarchist of the period and also Goldman's lover. But when he attacked Berkman at a public meeting and disavowed the *attentat* that he had previously urged, Goldman called him a renegade and lashed him with a horsewhip. She was not a temperate woman.

Richard K. Fox continued as publisher of the *National Police Gazette* well into the twentieth century, to the discomfiture of the godly, and New York City reporters continued to barter their stories for a weekend of his food and drink. A superb cross section of *Police Gazette* journalism during the Fox era will be found in Edward Van Every's *Sins of New York* (Stokes, 1930).

The sinister "Velvet Rooms" did indeed exist during the 1890s in many of the seamier establishments in the Tenderloin and on the Bowery.

For readers interested in crime and/or anarchism in New York City during this period, I recommend David L. Chandler's *Brothers in Blood*, Humbert Nelli's *The Business of Crime*, Richard Drinnon's *Rebel in Paradise*, and Emma Goldman's incomparable *Living My Life*.

J.S.